GODDESSES

2

THREE GIRLS AND A GOD

CLEA HANTMAN

AVON BOOKS
An Imprint of HarperCollins *Publishers*

Printed in the United States of America.

For information address
HarperCollins Children's Books, a division of
HarperCollins Publishers, 1350 Avenue of the Americas,
New York, NY 10019.

 Produced by 17th Street Productions,
an Alloy, Inc. company
151 West 26th Street, New York, NY 10001

Library of Congress Catalog Card Number: 2001092148
ISBN 0-06-440803-5

First Avon edition, 2002

AVON TRADEMARK REG. U.S. PAT. OFF.
AND IN OTHER COUNTRIES,
MARCA REGISTRADA, HECHO EN U.S.A.

Visit us on the World Wide Web!
www.harperteen.com

PROLOGUE

Our story finds our three Greek goddesses in a land unfamiliar—earth. Athens, Georgia, 2002, to be exact. Forced by their father, the great Zeus, and their evil stepmother, Hera, to go to high school, get good grades, and use none of their goddess powers, they must each complete a special challenge to return to their heavenly home. And while they know the Furies are in town to torture and torment and keep them from reaching their goals, they have, thus far, foiled the evil ones' evil plans. Still, the girls are wary, for it's almost certain that the Furies are, at this very moment, planning their demise.

Meanwhile in Olympus, Apollo, heartbroken and distraught, is clueless as to the real whereabouts of his spunky true love. . . .

ONE

Throp.

"Ungh."

Throp.

"Grunt."

Throp. Bounce. Bounce. Bounce.

"Ow! Hey, sir, I thought you said we were square," cried Apollo, who had just been grazed on the ear by a lightning-fast tennis ball.

"I win again," exulted Zeus with a grin, revealing a set of teeth as bright as the moon.

"Yes, again. You win *again.* Is this making you feel better? Because it's not really helping me." Apollo rubbed his ear, scowling. That ball had hurt.

"Why, yes, I do believe it is making me feel a tad better," Zeus answered cheerfully. "Thank you. Anyway, it's just good to get out of the house. It's been a touch depressing with those three girls gone. Thalia was always making me laugh, and I miss Polly's seriousness, her beautiful stoicism. And, well, Era, I miss the frivolity she brought to the palace. You know," Zeus continued, tugging at his beard, "I have been meaning to ask you—how are you doing, young man? Have my daughter's reckless shenanigans gotten the better of you?"

But Zeus didn't really want to know, and he didn't bother waiting for the answer. He just continued. "She's a handful, that one." He let out a long sigh. "Thalia, oh, Thalia. As much as I would have liked to have seen a match between you two, and, well, Hera would have loved it . . . er, Hera." With these words Zeus paused, cringing a little. "You know she still has some lingering green around the ears, but she is a bit consoled by the addition of that music room out of Thalia's old bedroom. Although I told her, I don't know how long Thalia will be gone, but she—"

"Sir, with all due respect, this is the very matter I want to speak to you about. This tennis game was just a ruse."

"Is that so?" said Zeus with a leering eye. He wasn't paying all that much attention to Apollo. He was concentrating on a tiny little lint ball that he'd just noticed on his shoulder. He just wasn't able to grab it.

"Well, yes, you see, I've thought long and hard," said Apollo, "and I haven't slept for a month at least, not since the party, the incident, the Scyllia, and the green ooze. Not since Thalia was sent away."

"That explains the lousy tennis game. I may be Zeus, but you are considerably younger than I. Beating you was a bit too easy."

"Um, yes, perhaps. Anyway, I want to speak with you about Thalia," said Apollo.

Zeus looked a little exasperated. "What do you want? I owe you for sure—just name it. Jewels? A higher title? A different daughter? What?"

"No, I don't want a payoff, no, sir." Apollo was a little insulted by the implication, but he carried on. "I do want something, though. I want . . . Thalia."

Zeus's eyes widened. "Are you mad? After what she did to you, to me, to Hera? Thalia will be lucky if any man wants to marry her at this rate. She might as well truly be green for all the men she'll attract."

"Please don't talk about her like that," demanded Apollo. Zeus's eyes revealed he didn't like being spoken to as such, so Apollo followed up with, "I say that respectfully, of course."

Apollo then began to walk and talk. "I've thought about this a lot. All those sleepless hours and, see, maybe Thalia isn't ready for marriage just yet, today or tomorrow. I now know it was foolish of me to rush into things without openly communicating my feelings to her. She was blindsided. I don't blame her for the way she acted."

"I know someone who does," Zeus said out of the side of his mouth as he conjured up a picture of his oozing, pussing, chartreuse wife.

Apollo was getting more nervous by the second. His hands were trembling; his voice even cracked. But he knew he had to defend Thalia. He knew others didn't understand her, not even her own father, but that didn't matter. He just wanted Thalia to come back home. "Well, *I* don't blame her, sir. And I think we just need a chance to talk, Thalia and I, and we can work this out. I think I would like very much for Thalia to be my—my—my—well, if she will have me, my girlfriend. And see, I think, no, I know, deep down in the pit of my stomach, I know Thalia has great, wondrous feelings for me."

Apollo twitched a little. He rubbed his nose. And then he said, more quietly, more thoughtfully, with a small smile, "Your daughter is the most special, incredible, creative, dangerous girl I have ever known. Your daughter is everything to me." He couldn't stop wringing his hands, rubbing them together, faster and faster. He gulped for air and then said, "I have come here to ask you to return her, and her sisters, of course, to Olympus."

Now the whole time Apollo had been making this speech, he paced. As he paced, so did Zeus, just two steps behind. The two men slowly switched feet back and forth. They weren't on a tennis court, in the traditional sense. It was more like a flat mountaintop on the peak of a very tall summit. And now they were moving around it freely. And while Apollo wasn't paying much attention to where he stepped, Zeus was. Right at the end of the speech Apollo went a step too far and almost went feet first down the mountainside. Zeus nabbed him by the back of his white robe and brought his feet back down to the dirt. Apollo didn't even notice. He was lost in his thoughts of Thalia.

Zeus did seem a bit touched by the young god's sentiment. He softened his shoulders. A small smile crept over his bearded face. He felt admiration for Apollo, who so obviously loved his wild-at-heart daughter. But then he said quite plainly, rather simply, "No."

"Of course you can, c'mon," said Apollo, who thought perhaps Zeus was just playing with him. Making him beg.

"No, I really can't. I don't believe they have learned their lessons just yet."

"They can learn their lessons here in Olympus. This is unreasonable. Please, Zeus, for me?" Now Apollo was really begging.

"Look, Apollo, the girls, they hurt more than just you. Have you taken a look, a long look, at my wife lately? Why, I daresay I've never, ever seen her this angry, this incredulous, this abominably hate-filled in all my days. And I have a lot of days, if you know what I mean." Zeus was trying to be conversational, chummy, almost, with Apollo. But it just made Apollo more frustrated.

"That's what this is really about, isn't it? Hera has her grips in you. These are your daughters, your flesh and blood. How can you do this to them?"

"Apollo, this may be what Hera mandates, yes, but make no mistake, I believe this to be in their best interest. They need time away from the vast comforts of home." In one sweeping gesture Zeus took in their surroundings. "Look around, Apollo—we live in heaven. Literally! Life here is easy. The girls were free to do as they pleased here, and they took great liberties with that freedom. Planning such a hoax, spoiling a perfectly good party, turning their step-mother green! Thalia is selfish. And the other two, well, they are practically grown, yet look at their behavior!" Zeus's face had grown quite red by this point. "One can't make a decision without the other; they meddle in business that is not their own. I love them all, but those girls have proved themselves to be spoiled and ungrateful. You of all people should understand that!"

Apollo's forehead wrinkled. His eyes darkened a shade or two. "Well, I do not. I don't understand. I don't understand how a father can banish his girls to foreign soil, with no care or worry for their happiness. With no one to watch over them!"

"Oh, well . . ." Zeus stumbled a bit over his words here. "Hermes will be taking notes to the girls from time to time, I assure you. . . . And, er, you see, Hera has sent a few to look over them," he continued, looking like he would be keen to change the subject.

"Who? Who, then?"

"This was not my territory," Zeus said quietly, almost in a whisper. He actually looked ashamed. His crazy eyebrows turned downward, and his face scrunched a bit to show his wrinkles. "She sent the Furies."

Apollo stood there, wide-eyed in disbelief. Then he screamed, "The *who*?"

"You heard me"—and this last part he really did whisper—"the Furies. They're posing as three mortal girls down on earth, at Thalia's high school."

"Oh, blast me! Oh, what have you done? What were you thinking?"

"They might not have been the best choice for the job, but frankly, the decision was not mine to make. Hera took care of it right after I banished the girls."

"That's just great. Just plum. No, that's it—now I demand you return the girls, or I will just have to go retrieve them myself!" Apollo's own handsome face was tweaked unrecognizably from anger. He was frantic at this point.

Zeus held back his laughter. He actually got a kick out of young insubordinates like Apollo. And Thalia. But he knew this was serious.

"You forget who I am. I am the great and power-ful Zeus!" And with that, lightning filled the whole sky. It happened every time he uttered those seven words. It was one of his favorite tricks.

Apollo crumpled to the ground and sat there in a lifeless heap. He was worn out, tired, exhausted with worry and fear and love. He gasped for energy, for breath, for words. "Please, Zeus, you are indeed pow-erful, great, even, I daresay, mighty. Please let me go and bring back Thalia."

Zeus looked slightly amused. Apollo wondered if it could be that he was responding to the flattery. Apollo thought it best to make the most of it. "You are in fact the single most powerful being in the whole of the universe, and you command respect from all corners of the universe." Apollo was clinging to the flattery as if it were his last hope of bringing back Thalia. "Your stature, it is envied by everyone, every single being, both animal and human. Your strength is unparalleled, your wisdom unmatched. And did I mention attractive? You are a stunning-looking fellow and—"

"Okay, enough. This is getting pathetic, really. I don't need some kid telling me how handsome and strong I am. But I do like you. I tell you what. I will make you a deal."

Apollo's eyes perked up. His ears twitched. He jumped to his feet with renewed energy.

"You may go down to earth. But I cannot let you go as yourself, for Hera specifically forbids 'Apollo's' earthly assistance. Therefore you must go as someone else. You must go in disguise."

"Sure, a disguise. Maybe a goat or an old cobbler."

"Now, listen, you may not retrieve the girls. However, you may help them along in their efforts to fulfill the challenges Hera and I have set in front of them. Once they complete those challenges, they are free to return home."

"Oh, thank you, Zeus. You won't regret this," said a smiling Apollo, who hadn't grinned like this since his and Thalia's engagement party. The one where she turned herself green to avoid marrying him (and, thanks to the Furies, accidentally turned Hera green in the process).

"But wait, this is delicate. You must listen and obey, or the girls' very lives are at stake. Remember, I forbid you to tell the girls who you are. If they find out, Hera will surely banish you to the nether reaches of Hades for all eternity, and I suspect my girls will never be allowed back in Olympus. Hera has the power. And as much as it pains me, I am fairly certain she wants them gone for good. Any misstep, any mistake, any reason to banish them forever, and I fear she will jump at the opportunity. The Furies have already reported some small use of magic, and it's taken a lot of cajoling on my part, and quite a lot of jewelry, to keep Hera from inflicting the strictest punishment. Do you understand the severity of the situation? Do you understand the dire consequences of your actions?"

Apollo understood. Down to his bare feet. His whole body shivered at the thought. "I've got it, sir. Thank you again for this opportunity."

"Please keep your goal close to your heart. Your purpose, Apollo, is to assist the girls with their earthly challenges. You may encourage Thalia to be more selfless, Era to be more assertive and strong, and Polly to find her own way, her own life—but nothing more. This is not the time to try to win my daughter's heart, do you understand?"

"Yes, of course. I will leave tonight."

"And make sure they're getting good grades in this school. Hera is chomping at the bit to see one of them fail."

"Yes, sir, of course."

After a quick bow Apollo turned on his heels. His heart was glowing, the hope inside him renewed. He headed toward the court exit.

But Zeus stopped him. "Apollo, there is one more thing." He took a deep, almost cavernous breath. "You know my daughters were sent to earth. But what you don't know is, I accidentally banished the girls . . . into the future."

"Whoa," Apollo replied, stopping in midstep. "Okay." He really didn't know what to say to that.

"And," continued Zeus, "it appears I have sent them to the United States of America."

All Apollo could muster in response was a quiet, "Huh?"

Zeus closed his eyes, bowed his head, and sheepishly said, "You'll find the girls in Athens . . . Georgia, um, 2002."

Apollo blinked a few times, bowed again, and continued on his way. He'd have to figure out the details later—this was a lot to take in. He had no idea what this new place or time would be like. He didn't even know if they would have goats or cobblers there.

But then, maybe a goat or a cobbler wasn't quite the right disguise for this journey. Because even though Apollo planned to follow most of Zeus's rules, he couldn't help thinking that maybe, just maybe, he'd be able to win Thalia's heart a little while he was with her on earth. And to do that, he needed the right image.

So the big question was, what was he going to wear?

Two

"Thalia, Thalia, are you with us? We're talking about socioeconomic criticisms of the various forms of the media. Do you have anything to add to this discussion?"

"Wha?" was all I could muster. I sat there in an excruciatingly painful desk chair in my so-called media class, completely freaked out. How was I ever going to get good grades in a class I totally did not understand? I mean, socio what? And what had happened to school subjects over the last three thousand years? Science was still intact (although it didn't rely on leeches as much as it had in the past), but now instead of history they called it "civilization theory." And music classes were nowhere to be found. Needlepoint, gone. Greek, gone. Philosophy, gone. And now I was sitting in a class about socioeconomic criticisms of various forms of the media, whatever in Zeus's name that means.

"Let's see if I can bring this down a few notches and engage you in the class at hand, Thalia." This was Mrs. Tracy talking. "What's your favorite movie?"

Movie, movie, I thought. Hmmm, well, I had seen lots of movies on TV. They played this one all the time. I hoped it was a reasonable response, gulped, and said, "Nobody does it like Sara Lee?"

"Uh, no, Thalia. I said a *movie.* They do know the difference between movies and commercials in Europe, don't they?"

I gulped again. How would *I* know what they knew in Europe? When my sisters and I arrived here on earth, I'd made up the whole we're-exchange-students-from-Europe thing because I couldn't think of another excuse. But the only things I know about Europe are based on facts about three millennia out of date.

Luckily the class just sort of laughed. They whooped, even. I breathed a small sigh of relief. Then I racked my brain.

"Clueless?" I offered. Now that I thought about it, I was pretty sure that was a movie.

"Okay," Mrs. Tracy said, her frown loosening up a bit. I breathed a sigh of relief. "Why is that your favorite movie?"

"Um, well, the girl lives in this amazing house. And she and her friends all talk cool."

"So, you like the fantasies of wealth this movie offers. That and the slang. That's reasonable."

I sat back and smiled, pleased with my answer. *Take that, Hera,* I thought. *I will too pass this class.*

"What about documentaries?" she fired off at me.

"Docu-what?" I asked, the smile no longer on my face.

People grumbled, but I didn't know why.

"I see the class is just wild about documentaries. *Not.*" And Mrs. Tracy laughed awkwardly. "Well, tough. Because that is going to be our next focus. We're going to make our own documentaries. And speaking of that, can I have everybody take a blank piece of paper and write their name on it? C'mon, right now."

Everyone moved real slow. "Chop, chop," she said. "Now fold them up and pass them forward." She walked to the head of each aisle and dropped the folded squares of paper into a giant sombrero. "Thank you. I will fill you in on this at a later date. Now, who else wants to tell me their favorite movie?" Everyone's hand went up, even of the kids who never answer any questions.

I knew I was from a different place and time, but this class was impossible. I wrote Claire a note and slyly passed it to her while Mrs. Tracy wrote some of the movies on the board.

Am I a complete dunce, or does this stuff not make any sense? By the way, nice skirt!

Claire had on a shiny, flowing silver skirt . . . with her cool purple sneakers to match her purple, spiky hair. She wrote back:

> *yer not a dunce.*
> *this is the school's attempt at prep-school-level classes.*
> *like it's supposed to gear us up for college or something. forgetaboutit.*
> *and thanks, your red flower pants are dee-vine!*

What I want to know is, how are you supposed to have a class on "media" when the teacher doesn't even explain what the word *means*? When I saw it on my schedule, I thought for sure it was a slight misspell and we would learn all about Medea's* revenge and the glorious stories where she kicks some serious butt, but no. It took me almost three weeks to realize the class had nothing, zero, nada to do with Medea. Probably for the best. There was that whole Medea-Jason-Furies-Era conflict over his virtuous love and adoration, yadda, yadda.** No need to be reminded of the bad times. Course, it's not like I can help it when the Backroom Betties, aka the Furies . . . oops, I mean the Blessed Ones . . . are just two classrooms over and

---

* A booty-kicking witch who was dating Jason, one of Era's first loves. (Era had several first loves.)

** Medea loved Jason. Jason's eyes wandered toward Era. The Furies stepped in on behalf of Medea, and all Hades broke loose.

we're all a few thousand years away from home.

The Furies. They were my real distraction in this classroom, not just my lack of a clue. How was I supposed to juggle school, Daddy's challenges, and watching my back for evil guardians from Hades at the same time? I still couldn't believe they were here, watching our every move. It was bad enough that we had to be so far from home, but to also have to deal with the pain and agony those girls wreak was almost too much. And the problems they had already caused us—Polly's pride being dashed by that poser Tim, that draining power struggle at the Grit.* We should've known they'd follow us here to earth, but we just didn't see it coming.

Tizzie, Meg, and Alek had this period at school with my sister Era. She'd come home crying at least half a dozen times already because of their little pranks, like zapping her with this huge cold sore when no one was looking and shrinking her shoes two sizes too small (they're already teensy). I could not shake those girls from my brain. Their sole purpose in being here on earth was to torture us. To stop us from fulfilling our challenges. To hurt us in any way possible. And they—they were apparently allowed to use their magic without a care in the

---

* Polly fell for Tim, but he was really in cahoots with the Furies, and he ended up embarrassing her in front of the whole school. But one night at the Grit, Polly's musical talents, and a little magical tug o' war with the Furies, put Tim in his place and won Polly a slew of admirers.

world, while we were restricted to plain old ho-hum human abilities. What would their next move be? How would we handle it?

I was up for a good challenge, but paranoia was beginning to set in.

Luckily my dark and doomy train of thought was interrupted when the VP, Mrs. Haze, entered the classroom and walked over to Mrs. Tracy. They whispered; they tittered and tattered. And then Mrs. Tracy announced a new student.

In walked a guy, the student, wearing a helmet, a number shirt, tight (ahem, yes, I noticed) pants, and goofy tube socks. He had black paint under his eyes. He was dressed head-to-toe in football gear. He was carrying a football. Even I knew about Halloween, and it wasn't for another month.

His name? Dylan. From Denver. That is how he introduced himself to Mrs. Tracy. And that is exactly how Mrs. Tracy referred to him. "Dylan from Denver, please say hi to the class."

"Dylan from Denver, we're discussing hidden themes in Jim Carrey movies."

"Dylan from Denver, please, grab an open desk, have a seat, join us."

I looked at Claire. She rolled her eyes and smirked. She was tolerant of weirdos (hence our friendship) but not when they were of the jock variety.

Dylan from Denver grabbed the empty desk three

rows behind me and sat down. Then he proceeded to scoot the desk, while still sitting in it, very loudly, three rows up. His final destination? Squarely between Claire and me. Everyone laughed. The teacher barely noticed all the commotion till the laughter.

When she finally realized what Dylan from Denver had done, she looked like she was going to say something. But she didn't. She just turned toward the blackboard and began writing. I, on the other hand, was mildly creeped out. Hello? Didn't anyone think it was odd that he was wearing his whole football uniform in school? Or that his uniform wasn't even from our own Nova High? Or that he just moved his desk a good six feet from its original spot to be right next to me?

The class wouldn't stop talking and laughing.

I guess everyone noticed.

THREE

"**And** then he leaned in and just stared at me. He had these big, black greasy lines under his eyes, just painted on. I'd never seen anything like it. And he just stared. I tell you, girls, first Pocky and now 'Dylan from Denver.' In this world, I am what Claire calls a serious geek magnet."

Era and Polly laughed. We were on our way home, and this day felt like one of the longer ones. I was ready to crash.

"So does he have a 'real' last name?" pondered Polly. She was pinning her long, straight hair up in a bun while we walked. With a few dignified nods, she was acknowledging the students who waved to her and said hi as we passed them. Ever since Polly had launched her singing career at the Grit, she'd become quite the celebrity. I would've been jealous, but she totally deserved it.

"I can only guess it's 'from Denver,'" I answered her with a giggle.

"You must admit, those football pants are something else, aren't they? Beats the robes back home any day." And we all laughed because while it was a very typical thing for my sister Era to say, it was true, all too true.

"An occasional tight pant isn't a bad thing, I guess," said Polly, "but I do miss the robes back home. They were more comfortable. And easier, too."

"Well, I like the clothes here on earth," said Era matter-of-factly.

"Me too," I agreed. "When we go home, I'm bringing every pair of sneakers back with me. I'm through with rope sandals."

"*If* we go home," said a pessimistic Polly.

"Of course we'll get home, Pol. We just need to focus. You're doing amazing in school. Era's doing okay. And, well, I'm passing. We need to remember to enjoy the time we are here. Besides, it's only been a month."

"A month! Already?" cried Polly. Her pale, round face went from sour to sick.

"You know, it hasn't been that bad. I'm a little homesick, just a little freaked out over my grades, and this certainly hasn't been the wild adventure I was hoping for, but this place is pretty amazing. I mean, where else can you just go and buy food, whatever you want, just buy it? And the television. Are you forgetting about the television?"

"Are you forgetting about the Furies?" asked Polly very defensively.

"How could I forget about them? How? I think about them all the time. I'm obsessed. I think about them even more than my stupid grades! But what can we do? We can't use magic. We can't call on Daddy's help. We just have to keep our eyes and ears open and our guard up. But darn it, Pol, if we let them rule our every move, we might as well be in Hades right now, washing their dirty dishes."

Polly looked close to tears. "I just think we need to take them more seriously."

"I take them plenty seriously. And so does Era. But that doesn't mean we should stop all adventure, all fun. If you ask me, I love modern mortal life."

"I love modern mortal boys," said Era. Then she added straight-faced, "And, of course, seeking out my own personal strength." And then she giggled quietly, as if she didn't quite believe it herself.

"It's not a laughing matter, Era," scolded Polly, who was in her most serious mood. "If we're going to get home, all three of us must complete Daddy's challenges. That means you, too."

"I know, Polly, but I think we can work hard and have fun while we do it, can't we? Please don't be so serious."

"I'm not being serious," said Polly very seriously.

And we laughed, even Polly.

"Anyway," said Era, "I *am* becoming more self-sufficient and stronger. I'm taking a survival class."

Neither Polly nor I could speak—we were too stunned. In the silence Era rambled, "You know, I thought the boys in the class would be wearing those tight pants, like that football guy in your class. But no," she said rather wistfully.

Both Polly and I found our voices at the same time, and in unison we both squealed, "Survival class?"

Then Polly asked, "Since when are you in survival class?" The class was notoriously hard. Supposedly it involved dirt and mud and sweat and a million other things that, while they may sound like fun, would not at all suit my delicate, sweet sister.

Era tried to look cool, calm, and collected. But her right hand began to twitter so fast, and her left hand started twirling a strand of her hair to the point of near breakage. She didn't answer just yet.

"You're going to break that hair off. Icky split ends. Stop. Now, what's this about survival class?" I asked.

"I've been in this class all along," she said. But the right hand kept twitching. Our expressions clearly questioned this fact, which just seemed to make Era extremely nervous.

"All along?" asked Polly very suspiciously.

"Well, mostly along," said Era.

I got hardball with her. "Since when, mostly?"

"A few days. Or so."

"You just joined today, didn't you?" accused Polly. "And why did you join, exactly?"

"Well, no, not today. I joined, um, yesterday. I, um, I told Mrs. Haze I was allergic to the mats in gym, and she let me switch. Anyway, what difference does it make to either one of you?" I could tell she meant to sound tough, but it came out sounding sort of like a question.

"Well," said Polly, "it makes a world of difference. First, you have to get good grades, just like the rest of us. And I don't see you doing well in this kind of class. Sorry. And second, you are a goddess, not used to physical labor of any kind, and I've heard that class is sweaty, dirty, and just plain hard."

"There is your answer—she did this because of sweaty boys," I said as I threw my hands in the air.

"Not nice," scolded Era, pouting her rosy mouth and crossing her arms. "I thought the class would be good for me. Like Daddy said, I need to learn more willpower. I thought this class would train my mind to be more survivalist, to be stronger and more self-reliant. I thought you'd be really, truly proud."

"Then why did you keep it a secret?" asked Polly.

We were on our block now, and Era seemed to be picking up speed. It was obvious she wanted to be done with this subject. We were only a couple of yards from our own cute little house when she got her wish. There was suddenly a blinding flash of light, followed by a humongous crash. A puff of silver smoke rose up from behind our house. Era and Polly looked at each other, their eyes wide. I got chills.

Then I started running.

It had only taken me a split second to figure it out. Obviously the light and the crash meant something big. And the fact that it all seemed to be coming from our backyard meant something big and probably otherworldly . . . something that had to do with *us*. I felt it in my bones, too—that it had to be Apollo. That he had come to earth to find me. He still wanted to be my best friend! Even after all the seriously horrible stuff I'd done to him. And he'd come to earth to tell me so—I just knew it!

My bouncy sneakers carried me around the bend at what felt like lightning speed. All my anger at Apollo for trying to force me to marry him and at Daddy for being so bossy and even at Hera for being so evil just vanished. Now that Apollo was here, everything would be great, fantastic, magnificent. As I turned the corner, I looked up toward our favorite tree, which was rustling all around. There was someone in it. The leaves were scorched.

I heard a moan. And there, right there on the

very branch where we liked to sit sometimes, was . . . well . . . was . . . not.

Not Apollo.

I stopped short. My shoulders slumped.

Polly and Era caught up to me just as the figure shimmied the last few feet to the ground. *Not Apollo.* My sisters rushed forward and tackled him in the biggest, tightest hug of all time. *Not Apollo.* Era showered tons of sweet kisses on his face, his helmet, laughing and chattering a thousand miles a minute. I just plopped to the ground, panting.

Hermes was blushing like crazy.

"I've never been so glad to see someone in my life!" gushed Polly.

"Have you lost weight?" enthused Era.

And a million other flatteries, which Hermes just waved away with his hands, saying, "Oh, nooo . . . stop . . . go on . . ." and so forth.

I waited a few more minutes, catching my breath and hoping that the love fest would soon be over with. Once the three had had some time to exchange their pleasantries and hellos and blah, blah, blah, I stood up and said, "Hey, Hermes. What are you doing here?"

I didn't mean to be rude, and I like Hermes okay, but while I certainly like his stories, he was no Apollo.

"Oh, er . . . hi, Thalia. Ugh. Um." He cleared his

throat, backing up from Polly and Era a little and straightening his armor. "Well, yes, I have to admit, this isn't a social visit, girls." I joined my sisters, and we all stared at him expectantly.

"The thing is," he stumbled, taking in our surroundings with a wandering and eager eye, "I've just come to check up on you, which your father has asked me to do from time to time, and, um, I'm to tell you that you must be extra careful not to use any more of your powers, as Hera was quite upset about the last . . . incident." And with this he paused and looked at me. So Hera had heard about what happened at the Grit.

"And furthermore, your sisters* have asked me to request that you pick up a few things, which," he said, pulling a scroll out of a hidden pocket, "I will read to you now. Are you ready?" Without waiting for a reply, he cleared his throat. "For Calliope, one lock of fur from an abominable snowman, three bottles of the best hair conditioner you can find, one—"

"Wait, wait, wait—" I said.

"What about the part where they tell us hi and say that they miss us?" Era interrupted, her eyes seeming to turn a shade bluer, if that's possible.

"Or say that they're worried about us and wondering if we're okay?" I added.

"Um, well." Hermes scanned the page, but I knew

---

* Don't forget, in total there are nine lovely Muses. We have six sisters back home in Olympus.

that he knew what we all suddenly knew. There was no part like that.

"Yes, and how in Zeus's name do they expect us to find an abominable snowman when we've got our own problems to—" Polly said.

"And didn't anyone else send word?" I asked, thinking of one person in particular.

"Or at least a nice care package?" Era continued. "You know, I would really love some ambrosia or some supplies from the Beautorium or even . . . didn't they even . . ." She stopped short. She looked like she was going to cry.

"Look . . . look, girls," said Hermes, shrugging and holding up his hands in a stop signal. "I'm just the messenger. And my instructions were to make sure that you were all fine, read you these requests, and be off. Now, I'm very busy. I've got to head over to your school and get your class transcripts for Hera. Then I really must make this delivery in Hades by dusk, and you know I have to deal with that nasty Cerberus* on the way, of course, which always takes forever. But I assure you, your sisters and your father miss you very much. Now, here." He leaned forward and handed Polly the scroll he'd been reading. "You three look very healthy and safe and well dressed"—he looked me up and down—"for the most part, and I'll be happy to report that to your father. You can gather these items at your own leisure. And I'll see you again soon."

---

* The three-headed dog that guards the gates of Hades and Tartarus.

Hermes stepped forward and gave us each a little hug. "Good-bye, girls."

Then, before we even knew what was happening, before we could even really say good-bye back, there was another flash of light and he was gone.

Polly, Era, and I stood there for a moment in silence. Seeing Hermes had been our first connection with home (besides the Furies) since we'd gotten here, and it had happened just like that. In a matter of minutes.

My heart hurt. Now that we'd seen him, I missed Olympus terribly. I *wasn't* fine. None of us were *fine*. We missed our family and our home. One look at my sisters' faces told me they felt the same way. And the thing that really stunk was, nobody seemed to miss us back.

"C'mon. Let's go inside," I said, tugging Polly's elbow. Sagging like a set of wet dishcloths, we straggled on up the back stairs, through the door, and into our house. Home. Our only home for now.

I dropped the scroll into the garbage on my way through the kitchen.

FOUR

Survival 101 Class
7th Period
Mr. Hawkins

<u>Supply List</u>
Glow sticks
Canteen
Bottled water
Food bars
Rope
Duct tape
Snakebite kit
First aid kit
Waterproof bag
Flashlight

"Here is the list, Thalia. I already got the water. Now, do you know what any of these other things are?" I stopped walking to take a look at Era's list.

"Rope, I know rope!" I yelled. This was sort of like a game we used to play back home. When Daddy had some free time, he'd make a list of things for us to find and he'd give them to all of us girls. We'd each scamper off in different directions (except Calliope, who thought she was too old for such silly games). Daddy's game was more fun, though, 'cause his lists had things like baby albino goats, pots of gold, and seven-leaf clovers (they're very lucky in Olympus). One time he added a female pink-footed leopard toad to the list, but everyone knows they don't exist. Still, Era came back with a regular toad that she had adorned with her pearly pink nail polish. Daddy laughed so hard, the nectar he was drinking shot straight out of his nose.

"Yes, I know what rope is. *Besides* rope. Do you know what a canteen is?" Era asked.

"No, but I don't like the sound of that snakebite kit. That can only mean one thing: snakes. Snakebites. Thank you very much, but I have had my fill," I said.

All of a sudden my head was filled with visions of Hera and I standing face-to-face the night of the dreaded engagement party, the snakes in our hair hissing at one another. Ick. I shook my head hard, hoping to shake away the horrible image, and started walking into this store they call J-Mart. It was far bigger and brighter than even the grocery store.

I couldn't believe Polly hadn't wanted to come with us. This really would have cheered her up after the whole Hermes incident. It was doing wonders for me, and I hadn't even started shopping. My older sister was just being stubborn, and really, who would want to miss this? But when we told her we were going to pick up stuff for Era's survival class, she'd just snorted and turned back toward the TV. See? Stubborn.

"Wait for me," cried Era, who was still just standing there in the parking lot, staring at her list.

"Era, grab one of those wheely carts like at the grocery store," I called. With only a few steps into the door, I could see we were going to be buying a lot of stuff. This place was incredible, a shopper's dream! Up front, they had makeup like Claire wore and magazines. Then, as we walked farther back, I saw they also had food like at the grocery store, and shoes and clothes and shampoo (note to self: Buy Polly an extra-big bottle—her hair has been looking a tad greasy) and dog food and towels and lamps and books and plants and so much stuff I had never seen before. There were hard things and soft things, bright things and even a thing that looked like a very own fairy's wand—it was shiny and it spun when you blew on it. Forget home, this place was heaven!

"Okay, I'm just going to start from the top," Era said. "I need a glow stick. Do you think that they mean a staff like Daddy's? It's a stick and it glows."*

"I haven't seen anyone walking around with a staff. I haven't seen anything even remotely regal other than the crowns they give out at that burger place, French Fry King. Maybe it's like some wizardry instrument, to put a spell on people with."

"But why would I need it for survival class, then? And there's a serious no-magic rule here."

"Good point. Good point. Wishful thinking, I guess. We should just find someone and ask them. Oh my Zeus, look at this, Era—come here."

"You found a glow stick?"

"No, but look at this glass jar of snow. Look, a tiny snowman is in there. It says Athens! This must be some rare Athens snow! Isn't it beautiful?"

"Oh, we should buy a whole bunch of these! Let's get six, one for each sister back home," exulted Era.

"Yeah, but get seven, okay?" I said as I wandered off.

"Okay. Who is the seventh for, Thalia?"

"No one, not important," I said, picking up a giant can of something called Athens Original Boiled Peanuts. I grabbed a can or three.

"Apollo."

"Wha?"

"You want one for Apollo, don't you?" she interrogated.

"Yeah, maybe. C'mon, we've got glow sticks to find," I called from another aisle.

---

* Daddy walks tall and carries a big stick that he thrusts into the sky whenever he's angry. Everyone stops, gets a chill down their spines, and goes back to business as usual.

But I heard her mutter, "Apollo, of course."

Yeah, so? I thought. But I didn't say it. I missed him, sure. If I didn't, I wouldn't be human. Or goddess, for that matter. So I think about him. A lot. I think about how much he must hate me for what I've done. I can't believe it's been over a month since I've seen his face.

"Thalia, look at these!"

Era had found these little starlike shapes that glowed in the dark. They had sticky stuff on the backs so you could attach them to your wall or your ceiling. They were truly magical and reminded me of home.

"Supernova! These are spectacular. Grab a bunch," I cried.

"We need to do the whole house!" cried Era.

"The whole house?" I asked. "Don't you think that's a bit, um, much?"

"C'mon, it will give it a touch of home. Polly will love these. Get them all," Era all but demanded.

"I thought you were mad at Polly," I said.

She just smiled her sweet rosy smile.

We still hadn't found anything on Era's list. But the cart was quickly filling up.

Finally we spotted a young guy wearing an orange vest. We cornered him, and Era thrust her list in his face, squeaking out a little, "Help?"

He looked at Era, up and down, and smiled. Then

he smacked his gum loudly and silently walked all
the way across the store. We followed. It was all I
could do to keep up with him. I kept seeing so much
great stuff. Something called a camera and all these
little, various-colored boxes with music coming out
of them, and golly, more shoes. And then I saw one
of those bike things that everyone rides. *So this is
where they get those!* I started to turn down that aisle,
but Era grabbed my shirt collar and gave a hard tug.
Survival had already done her well—she seemed considerably stronger than ever before.

Our gum-smacking guide dropped us off only one
aisle from my new bike. I was staring in that direction and contemplating how to get the bike into the
half-full cart when Era grabbed me again.

"This trip is for me and my class. We know where
this place is now, so we can come back. Now help
me, please."

We cruised the aisle slowly, reading every single
item, looking for something on her list, something
remotely familiar. We got stuck on "freeze-dried ice
cream." It wasn't on her list, but Era was intrigued.

"It can't be ice cream in this little pouch. It's not
cold!" said Era. She knew her ice cream. She had
already become very familiar with anything on earth
that was primarily made of sugar. She'd even gained a
little weight to show for it, but the extra softness only
made her look prettier than ever.

"Let's buy some and try it out," I suggested. "We've got the drawer at home with an endless supply of money, right?" It wasn't that I wanted to eat the ice cream. It didn't look appetizing at all. But I wanted to move on. And besides, the package was all silvery and space age.

I continued to read packages. "Glow sticks!" I shouted, like I was on one of those game shows and I had the answer. I had found them. They weren't anything like Daddy's staff, nor did they seem magical. Era grabbed the packets from me and started twirling them above her head as she spun around. Faster and faster she went, squealing, her new glow sticks in hand. I was glad she found joy in them. They just looked like plastic bottles of green earwax to me.

"Era, whoa, stop. Look, here is a snakebite kit and a first aid kit."

"Yippee! So do you think the snakebite kit allows you to concoct a snakebite? Because it would be so fun to make tons of snakebites for the Furies!" she said.

I got a chill down my spine that I felt to my itty-bitty little toe.

Just then, as if on cue, my three least-favorite girls appeared from around the corner and faced us at the opposite end of the aisle. They looked extra tough, extra mean, extra evil.

I thought about pushing the cart at jet-fast speed their way, taking them out like a famous TV bowler, but I came to my senses and realized we were one girl shy. Unfairly matched. At a serious disadvantage. And besides, I didn't want to lose my jars of snow.

The Furies walked toward us. It seemed like the lights above us began flickering. I swear, the music coming over the store's speakers soared to a crescendo. Each step they took was in unison and exaggerated for full effect like models walking down a catwalk. They tossed their heads to the left, then to the right, their wild hair swishing and swaying. Their legs looked longer than ours, their clothes looked better than ours, their faces looked meaner than ours. They stopped just a foot away from us. Tizzie stood in front, her hands on her hips, her legs slightly apart.

Meg and Alek stood perfectly poised behind her. They each wore a wicked smile on their face. It seemed like the whole store fell silent.

Tizzie spoke. "Oh, girls, what a surprise. How *are* you?"

"We'd be a heck of a lot better if you weren't here. In this J-Mart. In this town. In this world," I said with all the calm and cool I could muster.

"Of course you would. But that wouldn't be nearly as much fun, now, would it?" Tizzie said, tossing back her glossy, orange hair.

"You're so right—it is good to be among such glorious friends. I can't believe our manners, Era. We must thank the Blessed Ones for joining us here on earth. I mean, we, we were sent here for our wrongdoing, we had no choice. But you, you girls came of your own free will. Things must be awful slow down in Hades. That's a real shame. If things are so dead there, what are you gals doing wrong?"

Tizzie sneered, but I could tell she was annoyed. Meg spoke up. "Oh, we came here by choice. You mean that much to us, Thalia."

"I'm just saying, you obviously have no lives of your own. If you did, you certainly wouldn't have the time or the energy to be so obsessed with ours. That is, unless you were so jealous, you couldn't just mind your own business."

Now Meg looked visibly angered. Bright red spots were standing out on her pale, porcelain cheeks. She hated the idea that anyone thought she could be jealous of anyone. Anyone.

So Alek took over. "You think you're clever, but you're not. It's impossible for us to be jealous of you or anyone, Thalia. There is no one to compare to the beauty or the power of the Blessed Ones."

"Fine. Cool. Great. Just don't come crying to us when the Keres* themselves take over Hades while

---

* They execute all the Fates' wishes, which means that when they are good, they are very, very good, and when they are bad, they are *evil*. The Keres are just nipping at the Furies' heels, hoping to one day take over and rule Hades as their own.

you're gone. I mean, you're spending all this time down here with us and what has it accomplished? Sure, you've stalled us a bit, but you've caused us no real harm. We like a good challenge. We're ready. We're willing. And we are most certainly able."

All three looked flustered now. But Tizzie got it together one last time. "If harm is what you want, harm is what you'll get. We owe you, Thalia. And we always pay our debts."

And they turned on their heels and walked dramatically away, disappearing into a puff of smoggy gray smoke. Yikes. They always talk in rhymes when they are really intense about something *or* really angry. I couldn't feel my toes.

"Thalia, you were great! You stood up to them, you were strong and smart, and they were shaken, did you see that? You're incredible!" And Era hugged me tight.

But I didn't feel so incredible. I slumped against a nearby shelf. It was all I could take to stand up to them—it took every breath, every muscle, every tendon, every cell. I now felt completely empty of all energy, like I was just skin and open nerves.

"Thalia, c'mon, you were wonderful!" praised my sister.

"Era, face it, they are living and breathing to make our lives a living Hades. How, *how* are we ever going to get home with those three little witches walking the halls of Nova High?"

I shifted my weight to lean on our cart, and just then, the cans of boiled nuts inside burst open. Out popped three huge, slinky snakes! Era and I both let out a yelp.

It took about five full seconds for us to realize that the snakes were totally fake. It was a trick. A joke.

But it didn't feel funny when we heard the ghost of three very evil laughs echo down the hall, even though there was no longer anyone there.

Era's bottom lip began to tremble. My bottom lip began to tremble. We grabbed our cart and headed for the checkout.

FIVE

*H*e just sat there, smiling at me.

Humans are so weird. I wrote a note to Claire and slyly placed it on her desk. It read,

> *Jocko won't stop staring.*
> *Do I have boogers?*

She busted up laughing, and Dylan from Denver finally took his eyes off me—to stare at the hysterical Claire. But it didn't last. Thirty seconds later his eyes were fixated squarely on me. Again.

Claire passed a note back to me:

> *u r booger free.*
> *what's up with the football outfit?*
> *no other jock is decked out in that costume.*

maybe he walks into walls and the helmet is some sort of protection?

maybe he's a klutz who is seriously affected by sunlight and this whole ensemble is some sort of protection? at least he got rid of the ball.

I giggled.
I wrote back:

While he stares at me, the rest of the class stares at him!
He looks ridiculous!

Claire wrote back:

Yeah, but he fills out that silly outfit nicely.

I guess, I thought. *Maybe.* I hadn't really noticed.
Mrs. Tracy was rambling on about how teenagers are completely made out to be something they're not on TV. "Unless," she asked, "you all really are numb, dumb, and glum?" She went on, "If you just watched the *Springer* show, you'd think that all girls have giant breast implants."

The class kind of nervously laughed. I didn't get it. I'd never seen the *Springer* show. (Although come to think of it, I have seen some awfully large boobs on TV, like Amazonian.)

"That's why I have come up with the following assignment: I want to see your real lives, the gritty underbelly, the excitement of first love, the anger at figuring out who you can trust and who you can't. And I'm not looking for some sort of talk show nonsense. I want reality TV. Made by and for the students of Nova High. I want to see life through your eyes, how you view the world."

Once again I was lost.

Some jock in the back called out, "My view on life? So, like, you want to see how the babes all want me?" His fellow jocks whooped. All but Dylan from Denver.

"You will not make a mockery of this assignment, Greg Gatsby! This is serious business. Together we can show the television and news networks what teen life is *really* all about. I expect each and every one of you to take this as seriously as I do."

"Impossible," muttered Claire.

"This project will count as twenty-five percent of your grade. Blow this and kiss your after-school sports good-bye, Mr. Gatsby."

The boys in the back booed.

Mrs. Tracy ignored them. "Now, here are those pieces of paper with your names on them from yesterday that you placed in this hat. One by one, you will come up and pick a name. We will be executing these projects in pairs."

People shuddered.

"Let's see, front row first, please. Claire, come up here and grab a name."

I focused all my energy on that little piece of paper and Claire's hand. I watched her hand dip into the sombrero in slow motion. I focused hard; I concentrated on sending energy vibes to her hand to just pick my name, my name. It took all my willpower not to use my real goddess powers here, despite Hermes's warnings. Because I couldn't imagine doing this project with anyone else in this room.

"Well, Claire, who have you got?" asked Mrs. Tracy.

She slowly unfolded the paper. It could have been mine. It was folded in a triangle like mine. *C'mon, c'mon, c'mon . . .*

Claire's face went sour. "Josh Adkins."

No! How could all my positive energy and super-secret power thoughts have backfired? I threw my head dramatically down on my desk. I should've just used my powers! Just a teensy bit of magic would have ensured my place with Claire.

"Thalia, you're next."

I slowly dragged myself up to the front of the class, my head down. *Who cares,* I thought. *Who cares now that I can't get Claire?* I threw my hand into the hat with all the abandon of an asthmatic turtle.

"C'mon, we haven't got all day," urged Mrs. Tracy.

I unfolded the paper. It didn't. It couldn't. It stunk.

"What does it say?" asked Mrs. Tracy, with an extra-chipper note in her voice.

"Dylan from Denver."

I looked over at him. He was grinning from ear to ear. His eyes were beaming. His toe was tapping.

I went back to my seat and made six different faces to signify "ick." I mean, he was weird. Odd. Cute, sure. But mildly creepy.

Claire giggled but gave me a sympathy "ugh" look.

"C'mon, next, you, Jared, c'mon." Some kid I'd never noticed made his way up. "Let's move quicker, students. After everyone has a partner, you can pair off and discuss your plan of action. But first we have to get through this name thing. Pick it up, class."

Claire and I sat there quietly, sulking in unison. We exchanged looks of complete disgust. There we sat until everyone had a partner. It took aeons.

"Okay, now find your partner, students. Move your desks to get near them. Claire, please pass out these assignment sheets. They give all the details. In a moment you will sign out the cameras."

Dylan from Denver was next to me faster than you can say "spit." He pushed his hair out of his eyes and grinned.

"I know many of you kids love those new digital cameras, so the ones we've got may look foreign to you. They're sixteen-millimeter movie cameras. I've got fifteen of them, so that should cover each group, but I don't have any extras. I want you to think real life here, kids. I'm giving you each a roll of film. There are only two editing machines, so you will have to sign up for times. Shoot what you want, but remember, there is only one roll of film each, so be somewhat selective.

"Now, introduce yourself to your partner if you don't know each other. Spend a little time coming up with your 'vision.' This project is due in two weeks."

The whole class let out an "awww." Mrs. Tracy ignored it.

"Hey, I'm Thalia," I said.

"Dylan. From Denver."

"Yeah, you, um, mentioned that. So . . ."

"How are you doing, Thalia? How is your life?"

"Excuse me? I'm fine." He was looking at me so intently, and his eyes were so warm. But the helmet thing was just plain weird.

"So, like, we should talk about our plan. Our 'vision,'" I said.

"Yes, our 'vision.'" Dylan from Denver sounded very amused.

I was dying to get my hands on that camera thing. At least that part of the project sounded fun. Recording the events of a modern mortal teenager's life. Could be cool.

"So, I was thinking that maybe I can have the

camera for the next two days, and then we can meet up and I will give it to you for two days. You can shoot what you want, I can shoot what I want, and then we can try to meld it together in the end. What do ya think?" I asked.

"But aren't we supposed to work on it together? I mean, I was thinking. See, I think the movie should be like a little adventure, like two typical American high school teenagers on an adventure. We could go in search of gnomes or leprechauns."

"Gnomes? Leprechauns? What planet are you from?" I asked. But I had to admit, when I got here, I had wanted to see gnomes and leprechauns, too. Back home, there were so many stories about how earth was filled with them. And I did like the part he'd said about an adventure.

"Oh, I was just kidding about the gnomes," he said. "Yeah, and the leprechauns. No, I mean, like, we could just go stir up some trouble. Have some fun, see where the wind takes us, and shoot."

"Yeah, um, well, I like my idea better. Not that yours isn't good, but, um, mine is better."

"But Thalia . . ."

"Look, Dylan, um, from Denver, adventure is great, but I think we should stick to my plan." I just didn't want to spend time with him. I had no interest in boys. Besides, he was weird. "So let's meet after school in two days' time. In the quad, 'kay?"

He stopped grinning for the first time maybe ever, so far (from what I had seen). "Well, I need it first. I can't explain—I just do. Then in two days I will give it to you, just like your plan. Only reversed."

"Fine," I said, slinking farther down in my seat. "Um, can I ask you a question?"

"Why, yes!" He was smiling again.

"Why do you wear your football gear every day, all day? I mean, not that there's anything wrong with it. It's kinda funny. But why?"

He looked mortified. I felt horrible for asking. He said, "What do . . ."

Saved by the bell.

"Right. Okay. Well, see you, Dylan." I couldn't look at his hurt face. I hadn't meant to embarrass him. With that I got up and ran for the door.

So did Claire. We didn't stop running till we were halfway down the hall. Out of breath, she grabbed me by the arm and said, "When did Dylan from Denver even put his name in that ol' sombrero, anyway?"

Six

Polly here. I still can't believe that we're here on earth. That *I'm* here on earth. I keep thinking this whole mess is just a wrenching nightmare and that any second I will wake up and be back home with dear Pegasus* in my arms and my golden slippers on my feet. I can't stand the thought of the Grove at Helicon not being tendered daily. And who's talking to the lonely gaggle of geese that wander the royal yards? I daresay they are probably bored silly without my conversation. And I bet you a pile of coins that without my daily disapproval, Cleo** is probably spending all her time swimming in the lake without her clothes! I've got so much to do back home. Oh, but I am needed here, too. (And of course, required by Daddy and Hera's horrible law to stay.)

The same week that the whole Hermes thing

---

* Our pet flying horse.
** One of the youngest and most daring Muses.

happened, I decided I had no choice but to join Era's survival class, too. I'm far more knowledgeable about nature, the woods and gardens, than my sister could ever hope to be, and that's got to count for something in such a course, right? I thought, at the very least, that by being in the class, too, I could save her from a failing grade.

So I went to vice principal Haze and complained of a severe allergic reaction to the oil paint we were using in art class.

But then the vice principal suggested I just use some other kind of paint or pencil or chalk. I told her I was allergic to it all! Luckily I'd had a little foresight. I'd found some familiar, itch-producing herbs on the edge of our woods and made a recipe that I rubbed on my skin to produce a temporary red rash. Now I showed my infected hands to Mrs. Haze, who quickly transferred me into survival class and threw the approval slip at me as if she was scared she'd catch something.

I got to class a touch early, but Era was already inside. I spotted her before she caught my eye. She was sitting perfectly upright in a chair in front, every hair in place, a smile affixed on her face. She practically glowed. Nobody glows like Era. Even for a goddess, she is particularly luminescent.

But when she saw me, the glow disappeared.

"Now," she whined. "Why are you here?" She said

it with such pointed anger, you'd think I was a Fury and not her own flesh and blood.

"Listen, Era, this is for your own good. You're going to need help. You need to pass this class, and you're not cut out for such physical work, and, well—" but she interrupted me.

"What are you doing?" she hissed. "How dare you? I'm trying very hard to overcome my faults, to meet my challenge, but you! You're here meddling. Again! I mean, just because you are one year older than I, you think that somehow you have aeons more knowledge and nerve and, well, ptooey!"

She had a point, albeit a small one, and I had half expected her to be a little angry with me, but not like this. "I'm sorry, Era. But I think this is for your own good. How do you expect to get through such a class?" I snapped.

"The same way you would. Day by day, learning and listening," said my sister, still with a scowl pasted on her face. Her eyebrows were pointed inward and downward, scrunching her face into a wrinkled mess. She was still gorgeous.

"Yes, I suppose that is a good start." I had to admit that was a reasonable answer. "I'm glad you've given it a lot of thought, Era, but the hard-and-fast reality is . . ." But Era wasn't looking at me any longer. Her face had softened, her eyes had widened, and they were following a silhouette outside the door.

"Era, are you paying attention to me?" Really, this was too much. I'd come here to do her a favor and . . .

My eyes followed Era's eyes. And then the silhouette became a person. The teacher, to be exact. One Mr. Josh Hawkins, a stunning example of six-foot-plus maleness decked out in camouflage and army green. My sister was hypnotized.

"Oh my goddess!" I quietly announced. "I can't believe I almost thought you were serious—how silly of me! You're the same foolish little sister, driven by heart and hormones!"

"Uh-huh," she said, not listening to me at all, still staring at "Josh." All the usual signs, the ones I'd seen literally hundreds of times before, were there. She was fluttering her eyelashes. She was pouting her lips as if she were about to eat a ripe, juicy pomegranate. She was flirting outrageously.

Josh then spoke. "Okay, you bunch of pansies! So, no doubt you've all gotten your supplies for the big course. The runs we've been doing every day will help your endurance and stamina on this next set of obstacles." I tried to concentrate on Josh, but I realized I hadn't planned this whole thing out very well. I didn't even have any supplies. And more important, this man truly frightened me. "You'd better get your butts in gear if you haven't already," continued Josh, "because next week is your first test."

I like tests, I thought. *Perhaps this won't be so bad.*

And then, as if he were reading my mind, Josh continued, "And this isn't like the test little Ms. So-and-so down the hall might give you. No paper, no pencil. Just you and the elements. This is a grueling, five-mile military-approved survival obstacle course. You're going to start out on a fast-paced 1.5-mile run, scale the twelve-foot wall, swing over the swamp pond, and then it's hit-the-ground time. You'll crawl on your bellies under the rope nets and through the mud, and then it's uphill for one mile and down the back side to the finish."

His voice was deep and menacing. He more bellowed than spoke.

"Now, if I had it my way, every student in this school would have to take this class. You students don't take life seriously enough. Well, you will take my class seriously. And that means participating in my after-school workouts and some weekends. That's right, weekends. Those of you who've only been going to these workouts *every now and then* should not be surprised when I fail you right out of this class. Think of this after-school stuff as your 'homework,' people, from now on. Got it?"

"Yes, sir," said the class in unison. I even heard my little sister's perky voice in the crowd.

My knees were shaking so hard that I thought maybe others in the class might hear. Why on earth would anyone take this class voluntarily . . . besides my lovesick sister, of course? This sounded like pure Hades.

Fortunately, I looked over at Era and she did look a little scared underneath all that blind adoration. I was sure she would wise up. Then she'd simply quit and I'd quit and this would be behind us by lunch.

Josh was grabbing his bag and heading for the door as he spoke. "Today we're going to go outside and I'm going to show you all how to scale the wall. So grab your gear—we'll be out there for the rest of the hour." He was already out the door when he called back, "C'mon, you babies, get a move on out to the fields!"

"Excuse me," I called, my voice coming out as little more than a whisper. Josh stopped and walked back to where I stood just inside the classroom door. Era shot me a death look. "Um," I said, "I'm wearing a dress. What about those of us, um, in skirts and dresses, um, sir?"

"Who are you?" he asked, his eyes piercing a hole in my forehead.

"Um, sir, I'm Polly," I said, and then I sort of whispered, "I just joined this class."

He still looked confused. "Why?" he asked loudly.

"Well, because I'm wearing a skirt today and climbing a wall . . ."

"No, why did you join my class?"

"Um, I was allergic to, um . . ." But he didn't wait

for an answer. He just shook his head and went back out the door. The class followed.

I grabbed Era and stopped her from following. "Please, we've got to get out of this class—this isn't for us. Be real, Era." I was begging.

"Well, I dunno." She was being wishy-washy. "It does sound hard, but . . ."

"I demand it, Era—I'm serious. We're out of here. Now."

"Fine," Era said, throwing up her hands. "Jeez, you just shouldn't have come," she added, looking off through the window at Josh and the others and pouting.

"Well, I'm glad I came to this class. I'm glad we're switching back. Just imagine what would have become of you, your grades, our lives had I not stepped in and put a stop to this. Now let's get out of here, before Sergeant Scary over there sees us!"

I ran straight to the vice principal's office as fast as I could. Era sulked behind me.

SEVEN

It's me, Thalia, again.

So Claire and I got out of last period kind of early (I think Mrs. Wing had some sort of hair appointment or something to get to—she was eager to rush us out of class before the bell rang). I walked with Claire to get a soda pop out of the machine, past poser Tim (he couldn't even look at me), and then out to sit on the grass in the courtyard.

"That sixteen-millimeter camera is totally lame," said Claire. She was talking about our project for Mrs. Tracy's media class.

"No, really? I was looking forward to using that camera. Why is it so, um, lame?"

"Well, for one thing, you can't do any special effects—no zooming, no close-ups. It's totally Jurassic. I could do this whole thing with my digital camera and my computer in, like, a day. But no, with this camera everything takes forever and a day."

I had no idea what Claire was talking about.* I just nodded a lot. And smiled.

"You okay?" she asked.

"Cool. Yeah, I'm cool. That sounds cool. Uh-huh."

"Thalia, you're funny sometimes. Is something the matter?"

"Oh, no, it's just that I've got to get a good grade on this film thing. I'm not doing so good in Mrs. Tracy's class. And I cannot fail."

"Parents tough about grades, huh?"

"You have no idea," I said.

Just then our friend Pocky came driving up, honking his horn. It was off-key. "You girls want a ride?" Pocky yelled from inside his bright yellow chariot. Er, car. His Mohawk bobbed up and down to some music I couldn't hear.

"Yeah, I'll take one," said Claire, who popped up and looked at me expectantly.

That's when I noticed my sisters walking toward us, and I could see from here that they were fighting. "Go ahead, Claire, I'll see you tomorrow. I'm gonna wait for my sisters."

"Have it your way. Ciao." She jumped in the car, and they sped off.

"What's going on?" I yelled to Era and Polly.

---

* Back home, Hermes told a story so vividly, you'd swear you were seeing it before your very eyes. But that was the closest thing we had to a camera.

But they didn't answer. They were too busy bickering.

"Come join me," I yelled.

Still nothing.

So I tried this whistle thing Claire taught me. I stuck my fingers in my mouth, curled my lip, and nothing. They continued to fight. Claire had made it look so easy.

I got up from the grass, walked toward them, and waved my hand in front of their faces. They finally stopped long enough to look my way.

"You are not going to believe what your sister did," said Polly.

"Last time I looked, we were all related. Now, talk slowly, one at a time," I said.

Era jumped in. "Polly actually joined the class, my survival class, to check up on me! She hasn't learned a thing here on earth, still meddling!"

"Well, maybe, but just take a stab at why Era joined this class—take a guess, Thalia, go on, guess." But she didn't give me time to guess. "Because the teacher is cute!" cried Polly.

"He's more than cute, Polly, he's amazing, and I don't see what that has to do with anything," said Era.

"It has everything to do with it! It's your whole reason for being!"

"Whoa, not fair, Polly," I said. "Era might be a bit lovesick, and certainly she's ruled frequently by her heart, but boys are not her whole reason for being.

She's a caring, thoughtful, sensitive, fun-loving soul. I'm sure she has other motivations for taking this course besides the cute-teacher factor. Like what she said earlier about being a stronger person. Right, Era? So give her a break and drop it, Pol."

"No, we can't drop it—that's the point!" cried Polly. "We just came from the vice principal's office. Mrs. Haze says she's through with our allergies and our class switching and she forbids it. Now we're stuck in that dreaded survival class and we have to do this ridiculous obstacle course, five whole miles, and if we don't, we fail, and we have to show up after school and on the weekends, not to mention scaling walls in dresses! Argh!"

"What?" I asked. "I'm seriously confused."

Era explained at lightning speed. "Polly joined the class to check up on me, and she told the vice principal that she was allergic to something to get switched or whatever. So we went in and told her we now had to switch out of survival because we were both deathly allergic to dirt and she kicked us out of her office. She said something about not having any more of our 'tom-foolery,' whatever that means. So now Polly's angry with me. But it will be okay, I know it will. I mean, I don't want to do that military obstacle course, either, but Josh, that's the teacher, Thalia, and he is beautiful, and he even calls us pansies, you know—like the little flowers—although I know he must be directing that at me especially—and, well, Josh seems like he can be reasonable. I'm sure we can talk to him and maybe sit this one out." Era finally took a breath, and even though the words had come out of her mouth, she didn't look convinced.

"He's not reasonable! He's cruel. A machine!" cried Polly. "He's a bully, and he has no respect for nature or the outdoors. He's short-tempered and ill-natured and he wants us to scale walls in dresses!"

"No, he's not—how can you say that, Polly? Didn't you notice how kind and beautiful he is? I'm sure he'll allow us to sit out the obstacle course. Or he'll at least help us out. Don't say such horrible things about him, Polly, please—you're really upsetting me!"

And they went on like this back and forth, Polly trashing the teacher, Era defending his character. There wasn't anything I could do but tune them out. They were giving me a headache. I sat back down on the grass in protest.

And then I spotted the number fifteen through a bush. My film partner, Dylan from Denver, in full football regalia, wasn't on the football field with all the other jockos. He was filming something behind the bushes.

Wait a minute, he was filming us! I was livid!

I was all ready to start screaming, *"Stalker!"* at the top of my lungs, but I stopped myself. (Hey, I watch a lot of *Cops*.) I took a few deep breaths. I looked around nonchalantly, like I hadn't spotted him. And I grabbed my notebook. I ripped a few pieces of paper out of my binder. I grabbed a pen. A fat pen. And I wrote. I held it up for him to see. It read:

I see you

I saw the bush move, but I could tell he was still there. The bush rustled some more. And then a sheet of paper, attached to a fist, came punching through the bush. In big, fat pen it read:

I see you, too

I had to laugh. But inside, so he couldn't see my amusement. I grabbed another sheet and wrote. I flashed him my sign:

Stop STALKING me!

The bush rustled and then another fist, another piece of paper, and his read:

Stop STALKING ME!

Funny. Very funny. I grabbed a piece of paper and the pen. I scribbled, then held up my sign:

Bush + camera = STALKING

The bush moved some more. And then it revealed another sign:

Dylan + Thalia = A+

Cute, I thought. I mean, I could've been paired with that Neanderthal Greg Gatsby. He would've wanted to shoot girls' butts and wouldn't have given a hoot what kind of grade we got.

Then another note came out of the bush:

Dylan + Thalia = dinner tonight

Figures! I don't think so. I held up my last note again, sans any sort of smile . . .

Stop STALKING me!

. . . then I grabbed my bag and my sisters, who were still arguing, and started to walk home.

EIGHT

I have to say, I don't miss the pomp and circumstance of life back home. You know, the stuffy dinners in the great hall, the stilted conversation with all the boring old bigwigs like Poseidon and Dionysus.* But that's not to say life here on earth can't be just as lame. That night the arguing didn't stop on our walk home. No, Era and Polly continuously went at it once we were home, through dinner and on into the night. And the next day, after yet another round of boring biology and way too much math, not to mention the very wrong version of ancient history these people are teaching (including the foul notion that Greek gods are merely myths!), I was ready for something new—an adventure or a great battle of wits. I was thinking of trying my hand at these things called video games. I'd seen a bunch of kids outside the Grit going crazy over them.

---

* Although once Dionysus has a few glasses of nectar in him, things usually tend to perk up a bit.

But first I had to get the sixteen-millimeter camera back from Dylan from Denver. It was my turn to shoot, and you can bet your sweet turtle I wasn't going to waste my hours stalking the football player from another planet.

I grabbed my stuff from my locker and headed to the quad, where we were to meet. Dylan wasn't there yet. I sat on a bench and waited impatiently. I wanted to get home. Of course, Era and Polly weren't anywhere nearby, either. I noticed a little crowd gathering on the other side of the quad. Everyone was looking up. I figured I could be just as annoyed and impatient over there as I could over here, right? So I went to have a look.

As soon as I got a little closer, I noticed someone on the roof of the school trailer. Not just someone, Dylan. And he had our camera. I screamed, "No!" but it was no use. There was so much chatter and commotion, I couldn't even hear my own voice. I pushed my way into the crowd and found this: ten football players, all in their uniforms (huh, Dylan didn't look quite as out of place around these guys), lying on the ground, heads all together, producing a sizable man-made star burst. They were chanting, or rather grunting, and kicking alternate legs into the air chorus-line style. Dylan was on the roof, all right, directing them, leading them, filming them.

Claire grabbed me and said, "I don't know what

kind of statement he's making, but I'm sure Mrs. Tracy will find some deep-seated political reason behind it and love it."

"You people have some weird customs," I said, wishing I hadn't. I was always so careful around Claire not to say anything that made me seem too out of touch. Too much like a Greek goddess from another place and time. But of course, she thought I was an exchange student from Europe, so there was a little room for some confusion on my part. At least I hoped so.

"This isn't any American custom, Thalia—this is just plain weird."

"Right, weird."

"Thanks, guys, that was awesome—that's all I need." It was Dylan, calling down from the roof. Just then three teachers came running out of the building, yelling and demanding Dylan come down. Dylan spotted me and screamed my name. Then he actually threw the camera down, yelling at me, "Catch!"

I did. But not effortlessly. I mean, I broke a small sweat, diving for that camera. Another five inches to the right and it would have been kaput. And then Dylan from Denver took a small hop and flipped off the roof, spinning in midair like some wild gymnast in the first Olympic games, and landed, feet firmly planted on the ground. A perfect ten.

Not that I was going to tell him so. I was ticked

off. How did he know I could catch that camera? And where did he learn to do something like that? That jump was . . . was . . . was godlike. No mortal boy I'd seen could move like that.

Meanwhile the small crowd from before had turned into a massive-size crowd now, and they were all cheering and hooting Dylan's high dive. I took the camera, grabbed my bag, and headed out of school.

"Wait! Thalia, wait!" yelled Dylan.

I didn't.

But before I even made it to the steps of the school, he was there, in front of me, stopping me. "Hey, so did you like the human-star-burst thing I did? It looked really cool from up there—I think it will be grand, really showy, awesome, an A-plus!"

"Sure, whatever. You shouldn't have thrown the camera—you know that was seriously irresponsible," I said, very responsibly, I might add.

"I knew you could catch it."

"How? How, Dylan, did you know I could catch it?"

"I just did. Don't get so bent out of shape—the camera's fine. Listen, why don't I come over to your house tomorrow night and we can shoot this other idea I had? I was thinking, you and your sisters all dressed up in your favorite clothes, sitting on a hill, with the Nova High band playing behind you, talking about your worst fears and your finest accomplishments. Like a secret peek into the sisterhood. What do you think?"

"No, I think no, Dylan. I'm going to take the camera now and I'm going to shoot things I want to shoot and then I will return the camera to you after the weekend and you can have another day with it and then we're done. We're done with the movie and we're done being partners."

Before I had even finished the sentence, I felt I had gone too far. He wasn't so bad—I didn't have to be so mean. There was just something about him that got my inner goat girl all riled up. He looked truly insulted and sincerely hurt.

"Why do you hate me, Thalia?" he asked sadly. He pushed his hair out of his eyes.

"I don't hate you. I don't even know you."

"Then let's get together tomorrow night. We'll have dinner, you'll get to know me, we'll discuss the movie, maybe concept a few scenes. . . ."

"Look, you're fine, I don't hate you, but see, I've got a boyfriend back home and, well . . ." I said it without really thinking.

"A boyfriend? Really—okay, I can respect that," he said, and his smile got a little bigger.

"So where did you learn to flip like that?" I asked.

"Well, you see, I was born in this wild part of Mesopotamia and my parents, they abandoned me when I was a wee boy and I was left to the jungle, to the animals. A kindly female gorilla found me and took care of me like I was one of her own. I played with the little gorillas like they were brothers and sisters, and it just became natural to swing from branches and jump and flip from treetops. It was a lonely life for a little boy but exciting for a baby gorilla. . . ."

I was stunned. "Really? Wow!" I cried. How I longed for real adventure! And I hadn't heard about Mesopotamia since I left home . . .

"No, not really, I made that up. I'm just good at sports. It's in my genes."

"Ohhh," I moaned. "Very funny. I bet I'm the first girl to fall for that story, huh?"

"You are," he said, and then he bent down to my ear and whispered, "and you are also the only girl I've ever told it to."

His breath felt soft on my cheek. No. I shook my head. I had fallen hook, line, and sinker for the first adventure story that had come my way. I was starved for real-time action. And a little embarrassed by my extreme gullibleness.

"So what's your story?" he asked.

"Oh, haven't you heard? I was born to circus freaks."

"Right, I have heard that one," he said. Great. He'd been in school a week and already he'd heard the gossip. Good thing I didn't like him, you know, that way.

Suddenly I felt a chill down my spine. Like an evil

eye was upon me. Sure enough, I looked over my shoulder to find the Backroom Betties, aka the Furies, and they were walking circles around us. Nonchalantly, casually, but evilly. I hoped Dylan wouldn't notice, but he did. Oh, he did. He turned along with them, following their evil eye with his own arched eye. No words were spoken. I was confused. I'd never seen him talk to them before. Did they know each other?

Dylan grabbed my arm, gently, though, and walked me down the steps and away from evil. Still no words were spoken. I thought of crying out, "Hey," but the fact was, his grip on my arm wasn't painful; it felt strong and smooth and easy. It made me think of Apollo. And the night of the engagement party when he grabbed me and pulled me behind the curtain to give me a . . . a kiss.

"Those girls really are unnecessary, aren't they?" said Dylan, interrupting my beautiful moment and bringing me back to reality.

"I thought all the football players were crazy about those girls."

"Not this one. *Unnecessary.*"

"Yeah, that's a good way to put it—unnecessary. I like that."

"Like an old stinky pair of shoes," he said.

"Or a lingering infected toenail," I said.

"Or a big vat of snake heads," he said, laughing.

We both shivered, although probably for really different reasons.

✻ ✻ ✻

Now, who is this guy who finds Thalia divine?
To think her appealing he must be a swine.
Of course, it makes sense, this is rancid baloney,
We have a special evil skill to alert us to a phony.
But why didn't Hera tell us of this bitter surprise?
That Dylan is Apollo in mortal disguise?

Clearly he plans to help Thalia succeed,
So he must be stopped by a few evil deeds:
While Polly and Era bring their own fate to pass
By failing to pass that impossible class,
We will make sure that Dylan is sunk,
Their partnership ruined, and Thalia will flunk.
How will we do this? you ask of us three.
Keep turning the pages, and we will soon see. . . .

✻ ✻ ✻

NINE

"I think we should come up with our own diabolical plan," said Era. "That way we can head them off at the evil pass. I mean, you just know they've got something planned for us. We're like sitting swans here."

"The expression, I believe, is sitting ducks," said Polly. "I overheard Sergeant Scary use it yesterday in survival. Of course, he could be so very wrong."

Era threw Polly a biting glance. Then she said haughtily, "I don't want to be a duck. Swans are prettier."

We three sat at our bright yellow kitchen table, doing homework and nibbling on "dinner," which consisted of orange Cheez Doodles, peanut brittle, and our last bean burger, cut in thirds and drenched in ketchup. We still hadn't gotten used to this cook-for-yourself thing and preferred to go out to the local diners. But every night?

I thought I would change the subject. "Have you guys seen my new shoes?" I lifted up my feet to show them the sneakers I'd found under a pile in Era's closet. We'd been supplied with tons of clothes when we'd gotten here, and Era and I never ceased to delight in the rich colors, the cool fabrics, the different styles. It was one of the first things we took solace in when we arrived here, and it still always seemed to cheer us up to have cool stuff to wear.

Right now, though, neither of my sisters looked impressed. So I decided to try again.

"I shot some great footage for my media class today. I shot these incredible flowers that I'd never seen before. I even captured a bee drinking from the stem! It was magical."

"Did you ever think that maybe that flower is so commonplace here that perhaps no one else will find that 'special'?" asked Polly. "Maybe bees, too."

"Huh, I hadn't thought about that," I said. We didn't have bees in Olympus. The goat boys gathered our nectar for parties and stuff from far-off lands, but they never brought the bees back with them. Believe me, I'd begged them to many a time. They'd be a great thing to stick in the Furies' underpants.

"What is the point of the assignment, anyway?" asked Era as she licked her vibrant orange fingers clean.

"To show the average teenage life . . . I think."

"So what does that have to do with flowers and bees?" asked Polly.

They were starting to annoy me. Yet she had a point. I thought I'd change the subject, deflect the questioning off me and back on school and homework, where it squarely belonged.

"Hey, have you all noticed how much is just wrong in school?" I asked.

Homework was indeed work. Remembering false facts like, oh, that Ben Franklin invented electricity (hello, we had spotlights in the sky long before Franklin took kite in hand—it was called lightning), computing numbers that seemed to have no bearing on our past, present, and future lives, reading boring, endless works of pointless meandering. Earth was definitely cool, but school kind of stunk.

Polly concurred. Not about the stinking part, of course, because Polly loves school almost as much as she loves nature and poetry, but about the little untruths. "Yes, like the other day in history, my teacher was calling our own history "mythology," like it's just some sort of crazy story that didn't actually exist! I was livid. But what can I say? 'Excuse me, miss, but you have it all wrong. Zeus is my daddy, and he is as real as you are.'"

"I could think of a few ways to let her know—like turning her into a winged piglet. That would show her who's real!" I said.

Era sat there, giggling.

"She didn't even mention us," complained Polly. "Like we were some inconsequential goddesses or something. She ran through what she termed the "major gods," totally skipping over us."

"No!" cried Era. Only now was Era taking the conversation to heart.

"I know," said Polly. "And they have it all wrong. I mean, she talked a bit about how Daddy is, like, head god and all, but they didn't even mention the Fates.*

"How can you talk about our lives and not talk about the Fates?" I cried.

"So she didn't even mention me at all?" asked Era.

"Not at all, sweet sister."

"Rats! Let's complain! There must be someone we can contact, like that vice principal woman. Can't we tell her?" begged Era.

"Yeah, right," I said. "They'd never believe us. But it does make you wonder . . . just what else are they teaching us that isn't true?"

"Right!" Era was behind the cause now. "Like how do we know the square root of twenty-eight is what they say it is or that Athens, Georgia, is even in this so-called United States? I mean, had you ever even heard of the United States? How do we know?"

Polly interjected, "We just have to hope they're better with information from their own century."

---

* Three goddesses who control everything. Sure, Zeus is like the Big Daddy, but ultimately, the power is in the hands of the Fates.

"They *have* figured out a lot since our day. I mean, who came up with this television thing? It's brilliant, really, you must admit!" I said.

"And the chariot, er, I mean, car, that's simply divine!" said Polly.

"Yeah, yeah, but what about our own accomplishments? Why isn't anyone reading about how we invented the harp? I mean, that is an incredibly worthwhile and beneficial contribution to history." Era was whining.

"Yes, yes, it was, and we should all be proud." Polly had only a touch of patronizing in her voice.

Rrrrring. Rrring. Rrring.

We all looked at each other. It seemed to be coming from the thing on the wall Hermes had called an air conditioner. Oh, wait. No, that's the big box that shakes. This ringing thing was a phone.

Rrring. Rrring.

Our phone had only rung twice before. Both times it turned out to be people we hadn't met yet. The first person asked to talk to someone named José, and the other time they asked if I was interested in buying a subscription to *Sports Illustrated.* I'd asked for three. Claire had asked me for my phone number, but since I didn't know it, I just told her we didn't have a phone. That my host parents didn't believe in them.

Rrring. Rrring.

I went to the phone and picked it up. I heard someone in the distance saying, "Hello."

My sisters watched me, wide-eyed. They'd never picked up the phone before. I fumbled with the banana-shaped thing, saying hello back till the voice came in clearly.

"Hello, is everything okay?" said the voice.

"Um, I dunno?" I asked.

"What?" said the voice.

"Never mind, um, who is this?"

"Hello, this is, um, Dylan from Denver. Is this Thalia?"

"Yes. Um, how did you do this, um, I mean, how, no, um, hello." I looked at my sisters, who were both completely confused and impatiently awaiting word of who was on the other end.

"Hello, Thalia. I'm calling because I would like to ask you to dinner tomorrow night, Saturday."

"I told you, Dylan, I'm not interested." My sisters were looking at me with eyes the size of saucers and huge grins on their faces. Era even stood up from excitement.

"But Thalia," said the voice, "I really think once you get to know me, you will see that I'm quite charming. Just give me a chance."

"Um, look, I told you, I have a boyfriend back home."

Now my sisters' eyes got even wider, if that was

possible. They were holding back laughter. Era came over and tried to listen in.

"Look," he said, "I'm not sure, but I feel our pairing on this project was some sort of fateful happenstance. I feel a connection to you. I know you feel something. Plus you are totally adorable. Just have dinner with me."

I was blushing. And hoping that this phone thing only betrayed my voice and not my face. But still. I wasn't here on earth to meet boys, fall in love, or have dinner. And besides, I wouldn't admit it, but I felt that just by talking to Dylan, I was somehow cheating on Apollo. Crazy but true.

"Look, can't we just leave it at 'I don't hate you' and move on?" I said. And then before he could say another word, another totally charming word, I said, "Have a great weekend, I don't hate you, um, bye," and I put the banana thing back on the phone.

"What was that about?!" cried my sisters in unison.

"Oh, it was that boy, Dylan from Denver. The one I'm paired up with for that film project." I think I had a half-smile, half-worried look on my face.

"So, what did he want, dinner?" said Era, her shoulders all bunched up, her hands at her face in pure delight.

"Yeah, I dunno, I guess he wanted to get together. Crazy, huh?"

"No, it's not crazy. You're beautiful and funny and

perfect. So what's he like?" asked Era, all aflutter.

"He's okay. At first I thought he was like this total freaky jock, I mean, he wears his football uniform every day! But he's actually, well, he's kind of funny. I don't want to laugh at his silly jokes or his goofy behavior . . . but I do. I don't want to think he's cute . . . but I do. But hello, if we were to kiss, like would he still be wearing that huge helmet? Or would he take it off?"

"You've thought about kissing him!" said Era, more like a statement than a question.

"No!" I screamed. "Not exactly, at least. I don't know. It's wrong. I mean, Apollo."

"Yeah, you mean that guy you changed yourself into a green slimy pile of snakes to get out of marrying?" Polly said.

"And the guy you said you were only friends with?" Era added.

"Well, yes. Well. It's not that easy to explain, and you know it."

"Earth boys are cuter," said Era.

"Not cuter than Apollo," Polly argued.

"Anyway." All this Apollo talk was making me feel a bit queasy. "This guy, he's not exactly of this earth," I said, but I didn't know what I meant.

"It sounds like you like him," Era said with a giggle.

"No, no, it doesn't. It sounds like he's my school partner. For four more days and then no more. Then it sounds like he's someone I go to school with. Just someone I sorta know."

For the first couple of weeks we were here, I slept in the bathtub in the bathroom since on top of everything else, Daddy forgot to get us a three-room house instead of a two-room one. But after a while Era took pity on me and let me move into her room. This was where I retreated to now. I didn't like how this conversation was going.

And anyway, I needed some quiet time with my shoes.

TEN

I didn't admit it to my sisters, but Dylan from Denver stayed in the back of my mind all weekend. And so did Apollo. I thought about how they were alike (they're both strong and so funny) and how in so many ways they were different (Apollo is bullish and stubborn, and Dylan's just plain goofy). And then I spent hours trying to *not* think about either one. After a morning marathon of *Cops* on the TV, I decided it was time to stir up a little adventure of my own. I thought the first place to look was this room off the house. I'd heard it referred to on TV as a garage.

We'd avoided it until now. It was dark and musty and had spiderwebs. I hate spiders, and my sisters hate them even more. Still, I thought I'd brave it in hopes of finding something good amid the boxes.

There was so much stuff in this room. I could only assume it belonged to the previous owners, left behind for someone else to clean up. There were boxes upon boxes of unidentified junk. I was hoping there would be a bicycle in here. Polly just refused to let me go back to that Mart store and get one. Somehow she'd become queen of the credit card and all the cash. Which seemed pretty ridiculous to me, considering we had an unlimited supply of money.

After going through countless bags and even more boxes (and seeing numerous unnecessary items . . . a chicken with a clock in its belly? A painting of a single lemon?), I still had found no bike. But I found the next-best thing. I had heard it referred to alternately as a board and a skateboard, but I just knew it was my new toy.

I ran outside with my beat-up board to try and use it on the road in front of the house. Daddy had granted the world a beautiful day. The sun was shining. The air was warm but breezy, and it smelled like flowers and grass and pavement. Grinning, I threw down my board, jumped on, and the board went flying forward while I landed sharply on my butt. It was great!

I knew I could master it if I just took a little time. I'm a natural at most sports, won the Junior Stellar Sky Skiing championship three years in a row. So I ran after the board, placed it more gingerly on the ground in front of me, and stood on it. Steady. Good.

Then I propelled myself with the one foot while balancing myself on the other. Down the street I went. After just twenty minutes I could fly off the curb with two feet firmly on the board. Now, this was the most excitement I'd had in a very long time.

I figured I was doing pretty well, so I tried this move I saw a girl do in the school quad. I kicked the back of the board hard and flipped it all the way around and landed on it.

I fell on my butt. Hard. But it didn't matter. It was thrilling, downright exhilarating. I got up and did it again. And again. And again.

I skated around and around and up the driveway and off the curb and around the corner and back.

I had started to concentrate on the flips again when the board seemed to come to life. It felt like it had a mind of its own. It came out from under me with tremendous force and shot straight ahead, like Hercules tossing a discus, and went deep and straight into this large evergreen bush.

Then the bush made a loud, deep, "Yowww!" Talking bushes, oh, my!

I had begun to apologize profusely to Mr. Bush when I spotted an upside-down 15. I looked closer to find a football-pants-clad butt pointing straight at the sky. Dylan was sort of hanging there, dangling from the back side of the bush. I mentally took back all my apologies.

Then I noticed our camera, just hanging on the tallest, tippiest, tiniest branch, and it was about to break. I panicked. My grade! My life! I jumped up to try to get it but only knocked it loose. The camera came tumbling down the side of the bush. I made a dive for it but missed. Then Dylan's large hand punched through the bush and caught it, just inches from the ground, in the nick of time.

I screamed. He screamed. We all screamed.

"Where did you come from?" I shouted.

"Ow, are you trying to kill me?" he asked.

"Are you trying to stalk me?"

"Huh?" He looked dazed and wobbly. Yet he had managed to catch the camera. Impressive, considering the massive tumble he'd taken.

"What are you doing here, anyway? I told you, I don't want to go out. I told you I would see you in school," I said, sounding a little harsher than I felt.

"You don't have to be mean," he said, getting up off the ground and shaking the twigs out of his hair. He had a small scrape across his perfect nose.

"And you don't have to follow me around everywhere I go," I retorted.

"Following you? Following you? Why, I'm out filming the sights and sounds of our fair town. There's lots of excitement on your very own Castalia Way."

"Lots of excitement? On our street? I don't think so." Our street was just a collection of quiet, cute little houses, green lawns, and front porches.

"It's true, and I'm not talking about your incredible skating abilities."

"Hey. That was sarcasm—I'd recognize it anywhere."

"Don't you like sarcasm, Thalia, and teasing?"

"Hardly."

"Hardly?"

"Yes, hardly. See, you think you know me, but you don't," I said.

"Ah, well, in that case, would you like me to let you in on the excitement on Castalia Way?"

"I don't care, whatever. Sure."

"Your neighbors, Mr. and Mrs. Hall, are the proud owners of a dragon."

"Yeah, so," I said, but the fact was, I was all aflutter inside. We had giants back home. Monsters, too. And I'd heard a story or two about Daddy battling a dragon or three, but I'd never actually seen one with my very own eyes.

"I just thought you'd get a kick out of it, that's all. Apparently it's a variety called a Komodo dragon and it's totally illegal to own one."

"Yeah . . . dragons . . . huh?"

"And it can eat a whole pig in one sitting. And I'm sure it will spit fire. Maybe it can fly! You want to join me? I'm going over there to check it out."

"Nah, I'm busy." But I wasn't. And I wanted to see a real, live dragon. Maybe after he was gone, I thought. Yes, later. I could wait.

"Suit yourself," he said, and turned and walked away, the smile still on his face.

"Stalker!" I called after him with a small smile.

"Coward!" he called back to me. With a smile, but did it matter?

I picked up my board and headed back to the house. But try as I might, I couldn't wipe the smile off my face. Dylan's excitement over the fun side of life was adorable, even if it was infuriating.

And he pushed my buttons better than . . . better than . . . oh, rats! Maybe better than even Apollo.

✳   ✳   ✳

Thalia and Dylan, well, isn't that nice?
We'd love it if our hearts weren't colder than ice.
But since we are evil, our plan must go on,
We will not settle till Dylan is gone.
In the meantime, though, we have deeds we must do
Because from the bushes we've seen what we want to:
That Dylan, while godly, is a bit of a klutz,
Now all we need is to make him mess up.
What we have in store will do two jobs in one,

And all will be ruined, oh, isn't it fun?
Dylan will destroy his chance with his mate,
And Thalia will fail, yes, that is her fate!
The girls will be banished to Hades for sure,
And those simpering Muses will plague us no more!

✳　✳　✳

ELEVEN

Era here. So yes, I admit it, it wasn't the brightest idea to take this class. On Sunday, when I could have been in my best frilly nightgown, deep under the covers of my fluffy bed, I instead found myself outside, running for what seemed like eternity in the rain. No, not just rain, a dramatic downpour. I wore clothes that only Thalia would be caught dead in—baggy pants meant for sweating and those shoes with no pretty points or tiny heels—they were horrible. My "sneakers" were soaked through and squeaked with every painful step I took. And Josh, well, Josh hadn't looked at me once the whole time. It's no wonder—I was soaked to my insides, and my hair was flatter than a nymph's in Hades. I missed the Beautorium!

The tall trees around us blocked any possible small bits of sunlight that might have been able to squeak through the rain clouds, so it was just dark, which only made it feel colder. And you know what, it was uphill! Josh had said the first part was flat, but it wasn't.

Some of the more serious kids were ahead, and Polly and I were back in the last pack of students, struggling to keep up. Everyone was silent. All I could hear was the roar of the wind echoing against the trees.

"I can't . . . do it. . . . I can't . . . run . . . anymore," Polly said very quietly through short, deep breaths.

"Me neither," I said, and we fell behind the last group in an instant. We began to walk.

"I . . . hate . . . you," she said, barely.

"Fine, I don't care. Your own fault. Allergic to paint," I said. "Hey . . . do you have a mirror . . . in your pack?"

"What? I'm dying over here, and you want a mirror? Are you insane?"

"No, I just have a gift," I said.

"Excuse me?"

"I can see the beautiful in a bad situation. The beautiful in this situation is, well, if I can get a mirror and a little mousse and maybe a towel, is, um, me."

"*Grrrrrgrgrrgrgrgrhhhh!*" My sister had let out one of those primal wails, the kind that would be perfectly acceptable in, say, the Peloponnesian Forests, but here, in the empty wooded lot behind Nova

High, was totally and completely unacceptable. You'd think she would have had her earthly etiquette down by now.

"Polly, please, no yelling," I said.

"No one can hear us, Era, we've fallen behind the crowd. We're in the forest. It's raining and windy. And we're going to fail! *Ggggrrrhhhhhhhhh!*"

"So, do you have a mirror, maybe a hairbrush?"

"Era, my silly, vain sister, my mystically blind little sister, do you have any idea how infuriating you are? Do you understand the consequences of failure?"

"You don't have to call me names."

"Era, listen to me and listen good." She stopped walking, and I broke into a slow jog to keep up. "Your priorities are haywire. We are in the pouring rain, on the weekend, running for what seems like all eternity, failing one of our classes because you, *you* thought another random boy cute. So cute that you would join a class you have no desire in taking, a class that you have no business being in, a class that goes against your very nature, your very being, your . . . very . . . soul."

My hair clung to my face for dear life. Polly's just looked like it weighed her down, her shoulders slouched toward the ground. We began to walk again. "I didn't sign you up for this class. For that, you can only blame yourself."

"No, I can blame you," she said, practically hyperventilating. "I can blame you because once again, I have to take care of my sisters. . . ." But before she had even finished the last *s* in *sisters*, she knew. I didn't have to say it.

But I did, anyway.

"*Take care of your sisters*, huh? Well, I see you, *too*, have learned a lot here on earth. Because that is the one old habit *you* are supposed to be correcting."

She looked solemn. Beaten down. Utterly exhausted and totally distressed. I felt horrible. She then said, "You're right. How can I criticize you for falling back into your old ways when I, too, surrender so easily to my nasty habits?"

"Right. See. Now, let's stop fighting. Do you have a mirror or not?"

"Oh my *goddess!* You are insufferable! At least I realize the error of my ways, but you, you, you!"

"Look, Pol, Daddy didn't tell me not to care how I looked, he told me to not blindly follow others. And face it, I didn't blindly follow anyone into this class— and who says this class won't be good for me and teach me a little discipline? That is what it's about, right?"

Polly shrugged.

"No, that was a real question. See, I think that's the point of the class, but I'm not sure. I wasn't paying attention when Josh gave us that lecture the other day. I mean, his eyes are like the same color as the sky back home, and, well, he did mention something about discipline, right?"

"Eyyyyahhhhhhhh!" Another scream from Pol. Only this time Mr. Josh Hawkins was on his way to check on the back of the pack, aka us, and he heard her. He hightailed it in our direction. I tried my best to fix my hair without a mirror.

"Girls, what are you doing? Move it, ten hut! I need to see some action here!"

"So, Coach, that's an awfully nice shirt you're wearing, and your hair, it looks so good, even in this rain," I said.

"You're kidding me, right? Save the drama for your mama, girls, and let's get a move on. Neither one of you is taking this class seriously, and your attitudes better change right here, right now, pronto, do you read me? I will not hesitate to give you both a failing grade. Now let's pick up those legs and move it, move it, move it!"

I was trying, I really was.

I had tried to put a happy spin on this whole thing, but it wasn't working. I was still freezing cold, dripping wet, and totally exhausted. I was failing. Not just this class, but at finding my own strength.

I looked at Polly, who still looked angry, as angry as our first day on earth, but now she looked tired and dirty, too. She was trying to run, as was I. But we were barely moving at all. I wondered if I looked that dirty.

And then I started to cry.

TWELVE

While Era and Polly were at that survival class, I decided to surprise them with a genuine home-cooked meal. Like I said, we'd been going out to eat, a *lot*. More than anything because it was fun to try something new each time. I mean, the food back home was more grand—it tasted sweeter and hotter. But food on earth was pretty exciting. The choices were never ending! Still, we really needed to get the hang of cooking for ourselves like normal people.

I went to the grocery store and scanned the aisles. It was there that I noticed, on the back of a soup can, the instructions for making something called a mushroom tuna casserole surprise. It sounded fancy but only needed six ingredients, so I decided then and there to make my own adventure. A cooking extravaganza starring mushroom tuna casserole surprise!

Never mind that it then took me almost two hours to figure out what those six ingredients actually were and then to hunt them down in the store. It would be worth it when my sisters got home and I served them up a seriously gourmet meal. I'd even bought these fancy paper plates to serve it on!

So after opening cans and mixing things up and making a treacherous mess of the kitchen, I shoved my extremely fancy mushroom tuna casserole surprise into the oven for fifteen to twenty minutes. And then I sat back and waited for the girls. I figured *they* could clean up. *I* had had a hard day in the kitchen.

I sat on the front porch in this old creaky swing and watched the leaves blow around in the yard, but it was really too noisy, too windy, too icky. I miss a lot of things back home, but the very perfect weather may be at the top of my list. (Apollo has dropped a notch or two in the last couple of days. Don't ask.) I mean, this humid thing that Athens, Georgia, has going on is wretched. It's hot and wet and sticky, all at the same time. And right now it was raining, *hard*.

Just moments before the spectacular mushroom tuna casserole surprise would be ready, the girls stormed in, yelling and screaming at each other.

"Hey, yo, *stop!*" I yelled. They'd tracked mud into the house. In one brief moment it was everywhere. They looked horrible. They sounded worse.

"She embarrassed me to no end today. I mean, screaming and yelling like a—"

"She got herself into this mess and then she cried because she thinks she looks horrible, not because it was a complete and total disaster, not because we may fail—"

"And then to blame me when she herself joined the class after I told her no—"

"Did you know your sister is completely insane—"

"I bet she had a mirror in her pack all along and was just keeping it from me to be spiteful—"

"*Quiet!* Both of you, take off those dirty clothes, clean up, and get ready for dinner, without arguing! I made a very fancy dinner tonight, a beautiful mushroom tuna casserole surprise, and you two are going to sit at that table and at the very least pretend to get along, just tonight, and you're going to eat my incredibly luxurious mushroom tuna casserole surprise, every last bit of it, and you're going to make small talk and you're going to appreciate my incredible selflessness and you're going to thank me profusely and . . . and . . . *now!*"

"What's gotten into you, sis?" asked Era, totally calm now.

"I slaved over the hot stove to make this fantastic dinner for you two, to surprise you with my generosity and to show you how I can think of others like Daddy wants me to, and gosh darn it, you're going to enjoy it."

"Is there a freaky role-reversal thing going on here that nobody told me about?" Polly asked.

"Very funny. I just got into it, that's all, and wanted to surprise you. Now go clean up, c'mon."

"Fine," swooshed Era.

"Sure, Thalia, and this was very sweet of you, thank you."

"You're welcome. Now go."

As they headed for the bathroom, I heard Era whisper to Polly, "You do realize how ridiculous that was coming from her, right?" But I let it go.

They emerged from the bathroom fifteen minutes later. The mushroom tuna casserole surprise looked a little worse for wear, but I was nonetheless just as excited to serve them in a grand manner. We sat at our little yellow kitchen table. I lit the candles I had found in a drawer. I gave them each an embossed paper napkin (they had swans on them!) and dished them up a heaping portion each. Lastly, I served myself. Era almost dove right in, but I made her wait till we all had a helping.

Then I said, "Okay, now you can eat, and make sure you tell me how wonderful I am."

They each took a bite, and I don't think I have to tell you what came next. Rave reviews! Era told me it was delectable and said it was tantalizing. Polly gave me a triumphant thumbs-up.

Only it didn't look like they were swallowing.

They were smiling, but I had to admit, their grins looked rather forced.

I took a bite and understood everything before it had even hit my throat. My mushroom tuna casserole surprise was delectably . . . disgusting. It had the flavor of wet dirt and salty seaweed combined with a big ol' bag of worms. It was horrible. Worse than horrible. It was alarmingly atrocious.

We all sat there for a moment with a mouthful of wormy tuna casserole. And then, at once, all together, we burst into laughter, spraying slimy, gritty mushroom goo everywhere. Era's mouthful, a particularly large mouthful, hit me squarely in the face, which only made her laugh harder. I picked up my spoon and scooped up a big old wad of the sandy gunk and whirled it her way, hitting her wet hair. Polly fell off her chair laughing.

Era and I both looked at Polly and grabbed our spoons. Polly, panicking, began to scooch herself backward across the kitchen floor, shaking her head no at us but laughing all the same. Just before we launched our spoons of mushroom sludge her way, she grabbed a new box of Choco-Stars off the counter and blocked our attack. She then opened the box and in one fell swoop grabbed a handful of stars and chucked them our way. Dozens of little Choco-Stars hung from the slimy goop dripping from Era's curls. We each raced to a different cabinet. I grabbed a can of whipped cream, popped the top, and sprayed away. Era got her hands on the pudding and tried to smear us into a chocolate death. Polly, after going through the entire box of Choco-Stars, grabbed the box of Sugar Os and proceeded to pelt us with sweet and tasty little zeros.

It didn't last long. It didn't have to. The room was annihilated in under fifteen minutes. Our once bright yellow kitchen was now mostly gray gook. There was pudding dripping from the ceiling. We were covered head to toe in a gruesome mixture of sweetness and slime. We lay back on the floor amid our handiwork and giggled furiously.

"Yum, I love whipped cream," Era said, wiping a poof of it off her shirt and licking it. "It reminds me of the ambrosia back home."

"Who is going to clean this up?" Polly said, still laughing but shaking her head.

"Not me," I declared, "I made dinner!"

Era tossed one last spoonful of muck my way.

Yeah, I guess I deserved it.

THIRTEEN

"**H**ey, Thalia!"

It was Dylan. Calling to me from the other end of the hall. Didn't he know how to be discreet? Anyway, I ignored him but waited for him at my locker so I could give him the camera. We had to turn in the film tomorrow or our project would be late and we'd get a big, stinking F. I think that stands for *failure*. A word I know all too well. Hence this whole goddess-banished-to-earth thing. I could not get an F. I could not fail, not here, not now.

I tried not to look, but he was whistling a little tune. Dylan from Denver was always happy. He always had a smile on his face. Even when he was getting hit by a runaway skateboard. And he had such white teeth.

Just a few feet from my locker, he called out my name again. I looked up—I had to. He had a huge smile on his face as he bent down in football huddle position. (I'd watched a little Sunday football since I was in Athens. Tight football pants.)

"Twenty-seven, forty-five, fifteen, hut, hut, hut," and with that, Dylan came charging toward me. "The camera, Thalia, the camera."

I assumed he meant he wanted me to pass the camera to him. I handed it over as he breezed on by me. Just past my locker he threw up his hands, camera and all, in a victory dance. He made crowd-roaring noises. People laughed, even cheered a little, even though he hadn't done anything at all.

And then he just went down.

Like all of a sudden he was standing in oil. His feet just slipped out from under him. And down he went onto the school hall floor, a nasty concoction of sweat, dirt, and old gum. But that wasn't the half of it. The camera, our camera, came flying out of his hands, flew ten feet at least, and landed hard on the floor, shattering into dozens of pieces.

I screamed. A little scream, something like, "Ahhhhhh!"

Dylan's smile was gone.

"Oh, no! It's ruined!" I was still screaming. I dove to the ground. I tried to pick up all the little pieces, but several had shot halfway down the hall. It didn't matter. The film was rolled out, unspooled, across the floor, exposed for good.

"F, for failure," I said to myself, sitting on the floor in the hall amid the shattered camera. "F for freaking finished." I sank. I couldn't fail this class. Hera would never let us come back home.

Dylan was still splayed out on the floor from his fall. He slowly pulled himself up to a kneeling position and began to crawl my way. "Thalia, I'm so . . ."

"Save it," I said.

C'mon, he ruined my project.

And then I saw them. The three little witches from Hades, the Backroom Betties, the very vicious Furies stood at the end of the hall, whispering to each other and giggling.

I got up slowly and just stood there in shock.

I then looked at who was still on the ground. He looked so sad, so wounded, so sorry—picking up the shattered pieces of our project. I couldn't be mad. But I wasn't gonna hug him, either.

I looked back down the hall again. And suddenly I knew it was them. I knew it was all their doing, the Furies. But what could I do, stand here in the middle of the crowded school hallway and accuse the little witches of black magic? I'd only end up looking the freak. They weren't anywhere near Dylan when he fell.

The fact is, I wanted desperately to use a little magic—on the camera *and* on the Furies. But we could get in a lot of trouble for it. Anyway, how would I explain it to Dylan? "Oh, by the way, I'm a

Greek goddess from another time, so don't worry about this. I'll fix everything."

"I can't believe I did this, not here, not now. I can make it better, I will make it better," Dylan said sadly, quietly.

"How?" I asked hopefully.

"I could . . ." Dylan opened his mouth to reply but then seemed to think better of it and just shook his head.

It wasn't his fault. "What's done is done. Hey, I've got to go. You're okay, right? Probably a good thing you had that helmet on," I said.

"Yeah, I'm fine. I mean, you, are you all right?"

"Sure," I said. But I wasn't all right. I had an inexplicable urge to get the heck out of Dodge. It wasn't the humiliation or even the looming F on my academic horizon. It was the complete and total urge I had to kiss one Dylan from Denver and make it all better.

✳   ✳   ✳

Hurrah! Our plan worked! Thalia looked so disgusted.
Poor Dylan's to blame that their camera is busted.
Since she now hates him, he'll soon just go home.
Now, someone please get us a small pocket comb.
Era's hair is a mess, not pretty in the least,
like something all hairy . . . a wild wildebeest!

And despite all her efforts, she's getting no tougher,
While Polly continues to act like her mother.
They're failing their challenges and their class, too.
It's so easy, we almost have nothing to do.
So let's take a break and go celebrate in style,
Let's coerce Mr. Hawkins to make his class run ten miles!

*   *   *

FOURTEEN

I thought about him throughout Bio. Which was hard, considering my very shy lab partner, Wilma, and I were dissecting a frog. Well, I wasn't dissecting a frog. I couldn't bring myself to do it. I have a pet frog back home named Wilbur who helps me with my most foolish charms. I took the F. This was becoming a habit of mine.

Still, Mr. Z. made me watch and participate even though I wouldn't actually take knife to hand. Trying to figure out why I had wanted to kiss a goofy football jock in the middle of the school hallway while watching someone remove frog gizzards with a rusty pair of tweezers wasn't easy. Yet I wasn't all that distracted by the toad.

At lunch I slowly made my way to Claire, across the quad. But before I could reach her and the bench,

I saw him. Dylan was sitting alone in the courtyard, and he was sulking. Or at least that's what it looked like. He most certainly wasn't smiling like his usual self. Could he be this upset over the F?

I stood there for a moment. Maybe three. Trying to figure out what to do, if anything. I mean, an F. I have to get good grades, or I don't have a chance of getting home. But Dylan looked like he had as much to lose as I did. He looked devastated. *Maybe he's got parents who will be furious with him over something like this, like Claire's,* I thought.

I walked in his direction. I still didn't know what I was going to say. Till I said it.

"Hey. Who cares about a silly documentary on some ancient camera for a hippie teacher, anyway, right?"

"I'm real sorry, Thalia. I didn't mean . . ."

"I know," I said. "No problem. Really. An F, hey, we'll live, right?"

"I didn't want to let you down."

"You didn't let me down. It was an accident."

"A colossal one. Really, I am so very sorry. . . ."

"Stop with the apologies already."

"But it was such a good film. I know we would've gotten an A-plus. I mean, your bee stuff was great, and my human star burst! And I'd shot footage of that Komodo dragon, although admittedly the thing was a bit smaller than I'd expected."

"Look, maybe we can talk to Mrs. Tracy and—"

"Tried it," Dylan interrupted. "She heard all about the accident and how it happened. She won't give us any extra time, and she said we're lucky not to get an automatic F just for breaking the camera in the first place."

"Oh. Okay, then, um . . ." I racked my brain for a few seconds. Dylan's shoulders slumped about an inch more, if that was possible. "Hey! Claire mentioned something about having a video camera and computer and making movies. Why don't I see if I can borrow Claire's video camera? Maybe we could throw something together quick. Claire said this project would only take a day on her camera. It wouldn't be on Mrs. Tracy's precious sixteen millimeter, but she might appreciate our resourcefulness. It's worth a try, no?"

"Wow. That would be great. You're a genius."

"Sometimes."

"Well, thanks for including me, Thalia. I know you could probably do this on your own and just leave me to hang in Tracy's class. It's very sweet of you."

"Don't thank me. I need your help. I couldn't pull this off by myself. And besides, you are my partner. I'll meet you here after school, okay?"

"Sure. You want to join me for lunch?"

"Well, um, see, Claire's waiting for me over there. I gotta go. But right here, after school, okay?"

"Wouldn't miss it for anything in the universe," he said with a very, very mischievous grin.

FIFTEEN

Claire and I met Dylan at the bench. He looked eager, sweet, gorgeous. It was awkward, the walk to Claire's house. We didn't talk much. Dylan asked a few questions; I gave one-word answers at best. It just felt weird somehow with Claire there. Less comfortable. Stiff.

When we got to her house, Claire loaned us her video camera without much instruction besides pointing out the big red button (that means record) and the smaller button that allows you to zoom in on someone's nostril hairs if you so desire. After that, we were off.

First stop: the park. We chased birds and interviewed the old men who were playing chess out by the fountain. Dylan asked them, "What was the best day of your life?" And one man in a fuzzy-collared

shirt said, "Why, today, of course!" He asked another
to tell us about the best adventure he had ever been
on, and this man with a big red nose told us this
incredible story about how he met his wife of forty-
two years in a Paris café. But there weren't any
teenagers around, so after a while we left.

We then headed on over to the Pile, this crazy
used clothing store that literally has piles of clothes.
All the people working there were our age.

We asked if they would be in our movie. They
just sort of shrugged yes. But then, when we turned
the little camera on them and asked them questions
like, "What do you do after work, with your
friends?" or, "What is the most important thing you
own?" they totally loosened up and talked endlessly.

After we shot tons of footage of the customers
and the employees, we shopped!

When no one was looking, I climbed up on the
biggest pile of all and then sank down in the mountain of clothes. We tried on loud shirts and crazy
ties while filming each other. Dylan's hair kept
falling in his eyes, and he brushed it away each time
with this little smirk. And he bought this velvety,
raspberry red scarf for me, and when I tried to tell
him no, he said I had to take it, I looked too good
in red not to.

We went to a café and a grocery store and interviewed more teenagers.

"What is the most important political cause to you right now?"

"What school subject do you think is useless?"

"What do you wish they taught in high school?"

"Who is your best friend and why?"

Then we went to the university campus, where there was a spectacularly beautiful statue of my cousin Athena. Both Athens (Greece and Georgia) are named after her. I was stunned. I had lived here now for over a month, and I had not known this was here.

"Why did you bring me here?" I asked Dylan, who had led the way.

"I thought you would like it. You do, don't you?" he said.

"Yeah, this is a gorgeous statue. Wow, thank you."

He grabbed my hand and walked me closer. His hand felt so strong and yet soft. Almost tingly. "Here, stand there in front of it," he said. "I'm going to ask *you* a question now."

"Sure, I guess," I said, staring up at Athena's beautiful face.

Athena is spectacular, strong, and smart. She sends the best postcards, from exotic locations around the universe. Standing in front of her statue, I wondered if she had ever been here. I almost felt her presence, although I knew that was ridiculous. She was only, like, thousands of years and a whole host of miles away.

"Why is Athena your hero?"

"What, my hero?" How did he know?

He turned the camera on me and repeated himself, "Thalia, why is Athena your hero?"

"Because she is the strongest woman ever to walk this earth. She is good and kind and doesn't take anything from anyone. She is her own woman."

I started to feel sad. I missed home.

"I think we've got enough," I said. Fact is, being there next to the statue made me think of Apollo, and I actually felt guilty for having such a great time with Dylan. I felt this rush of pain in my heart at the thought that Apollo might never speak to me again. And here I was, on earth, with a mortal boy, having fun. I was horrible. I had to get my mind back to work; I had to concentrate on saving my grade and getting back home. "Stop the tape. Let's get back to Claire's and edit this thing—we don't have all night."

"Right, okay then."

We walked back to Claire's. I was once again quiet. I didn't want to feel anything for this guy. I mean, here we were, walking down the street, and he's decked out head to toe in football gear. Again. He obviously had some weird obsession with this uniform, yet nobody had ever said much of anything about it to him. I figured it was because he was so charming.

"Hey, guys," said Claire when we got to her door.

"Come on up. My room is upstairs—that's where my computer is. I'll get you some drinks and make some snacks. You can just get to work if you like—the computer is on." And she went off to the kitchen. As we walked up the stairs, I whispered to Dylan, "Do you know how to work a computer?" and he said, "Not really. I guess you don't, either?"

This was going to be a long night.

We sat in Claire's room in silence, waiting for her to come back. When she arrived, she had a tray of lemonade and fluffy marshmallow treats.

"Neither one of you knows how to work this thing, do you?" she asked.

"Was it that obvious?" I asked.

"Sheesh, I had no idea that Athens, Georgia, had such a computer tech leg up on the rest of the world. All right, I'm going to give you the crash course because I have my own tedious high school work to do this evening. So c'mon, grab a Krispie Treat and pull up a chair."

After giving us our little lesson, Claire climbed onto her bed with her calculus books. Dylan and I didn't speak much at first, other than to argue over who had control of the mouse. But once we started seeing the fruits of our camera work, we perked up a bit. There was Dylan, wearing a huge curly black wig in the Pile, and me near the statue of Athena. The old men at the park, the teenagers at the café and the grocery store. It was miraculous how it was all just there, better even than TV because it was us. Well, not "us." But it was Dylan and me, even if we weren't together.

Before we knew it, it was ten at night and Claire was fast asleep. Her mom had come in and checked on us earlier, but all parental interruption stopped around eight. We had so lost track of the time. But the thing was, I wasn't tired. We figured out how to add a layer of sound, and so we took one of Claire's CDs, popped it in the computer, and added a little music to the movie. We repeated the old man telling us today was his most favorite day over and over at the end. It wasn't as flashy or wild as our first film. But it was really great, like something I would see on TV. We were geniuses.

But finally, in the end, tired geniuses. We weren't finished till one in the morning. And when I noticed the time, I panicked. "Isn't your mom or dad going to be mad or worried about you?" I asked.

"No, they're cool—they know I'm out with you," he said.

"With me. Um, we're not 'out,' we're working."

"Whatever," he said with a little grin.

"I mean, so what, that makes it okay for you to be out because you're with me?"

"Yep."

"But they don't even know me," I said.

"But they feel like they do. What about your host parents?"

"Oh, I told them I was sleeping here, at Claire's." Which was a lie. And now Claire was conked out, her parents long ago asleep.

"Did you? Okay. Well, I suppose I should leave you to get some sleep, then."

"Yeah, probably."

Dylan said, "We made an awesome movie, you and I."

"Yeah, it was probably fate that you busted the camera, huh?"

"Fate. Yes, I would definitely say it was fate." He was just staring at me, his eyes all bright even though it was some ungodly hour of the night.

"I just mean, we made a better movie in the end, probably. I mean, it's all about the grade, right?"

"Absolutely," he whispered, smiling at me and shaking his head slightly.

He was getting closer to me, still staring at me, smiling at me. I felt my stomach drop. He brushed a wisp of hair out of my eyes and tucked it behind my ear. Softly he said, "The grade, it was all about the grade," and then he was only inches, centimeters from my face. I panicked.

"I think you should go, I mean your parents, they must be, so, um," I stammered, and stood up, backed away.

He was still smiling.

"Yeah, okay," he said.

I couldn't look at him. I walked over to the other

side of the room and tossed him his jacket without even watching where it landed.

"Okay, then," he said, "I'm leaving. Hey, Thalia, ask me what was the best day of my life."

I didn't say anything.

"C'mon, just ask me," he said in a teasing voice, his smile as big as ever.

"What was the best day of your life," I asked, without even looking at him.

"Why, today, of course!" And he laughed a little laugh.

I didn't say anything.

He turned around and walked to the door.

But just before he made it through, I said, "Do you want to have dinner at my house tomorrow night? I make a mean mushroom tuna casserole surprise."

SIXTEEN

"So tell us again, why did you stay over at Claire's house?" asked Polly. She was being very motherly, and I didn't appreciate it at the moment. I did appreciate the fact that she'd let us go out to the Donut Hole for breakfast before school, though.

"I had homework that has to be turned in today. I mean, well, you know how Dylan ruined our film and our camera yesterday, so we had to shoot a new film, so Claire lent us her video camera, well, her parents', actually, and we shot this movie and then we had to edit it on a computer. Man, those things are cool—you've got to check this thing out and . . ."

"Oh, we've got computers in my English lab," said Era with a mouth full of creme.

"Do you know how to use them?" I asked in

wonder. Could my sister be adapting quicker to modern earth life than me? Not possible.

"Yeah, I thought you all had them in your classes."

"How did I get so left out?" Polly whined. "What does it do?"

"Well, Claire's makes movies. And that's what we did, we made a movie. Hey, did you know there's a statue of Athena at the university?"

"Ommpfh, yeah, I saw a picture of it in my art class," said Era through a glob of chocolate pudding.

"Why didn't you tell us?" I asked.

"I dunno, I didn't think of it."

"Hello, big concrete statue of our cousin in this random town thousands of years away and you don't think to mention it?" I asked.

"Well, um, not really, yum." She was licking her fingers.

"So was Dylan there with you at Claire's?" Polly asked. Her eyebrows were raised in a sort of sideways question mark.

"Well, not all night, if that's what you mean." I felt the heat rising to my cheeks. I tried to stop it. I willed it to stay deep-seated and far away from my face.

It was no use.

"Woo wike him, huh?" said Era, chomping.

"Don't be ridiculous. We're just friends." And then this part I sorta mumbled. "But he is coming over for dinner tonight."

"What?" Polly said. "You surely don't like him, then, because you could kill him with your so-called cooking. And the parents thing, what are you going to tell him?" Era just sat way back in her chair and grinned. I shrugged. I'd think of something.

"Well, you know, we won't be around for dinner this evening," said Polly.

"Why not?"

"Don't ask, please, I don't want to talk about it," said Era.

"Of course you don't want to talk about it—it only reminds you of your foolish behavior," Polly said, and then she turned to me. "Our obstacle race is tonight. At six." And then I heard an audible groan. From both my sisters.

"What? First on a Sunday and now after school? Doesn't he know you have lives?"

They both just stared at me with that "duh" look.

"Mr. Hawkins is a sadistic, evil beastling from the nether reaches of Hades, I'm sure of it," complained Polly.

"He is not! Don't talk about him like that! Josh is just very serious. He thinks school should extend to all hours of the week, that's all," cried Era.

"Don't start with me, Era. You want to have a crush on him, fine. You want to act like a fool, prancing through mud and carrying a backpack full of makeup, fine. But don't you dare tell me that man is 'cute' or 'warm' or 'fuzzy.' He isn't any of those things. And the day I have to hold my tongue on the matter is the day I am forced to hold my tongue forever!"

"Well, that is just fine by me. I don't think I want to talk to you anymore, anyway."

I tried reasoning with them. "Girls, c'mon, stop this, you're both being unreasonable."

"I'm not the unreasonable one," said Polly. "Your sister over there is."

"Please, Thalia, tell your sister, *she* is being the fool," said Era.

"I'm not gonna tell her anything of the sort—she's sitting right here. This is ridiculous."

"Don't talk to me about ridiculous, Thalia," Polly said, looking around at the customers nearby and lowering her voice to a hiss. "Inviting a boy over for dinner? *A*—I thought you wanted to stay away from them, *B*"—and this she whispered—"we don't have any parents, and *C*—you can't cook."

"I can agree with you there," said Era.

"Don't talk to me," said Polly.

Well, this was fun. The only thing they agreed on was my poor cooking skills.

"I thought my food brought us together," I said.

"Hardly," replied Polly.

"I'm outta here. You guys can just walk without me," said Era, and with that she grabbed her stuff and took off through the exit.

Polly wasn't far behind. "Me too." And she got up and left, only in the opposite direction, through the other exit.

That left me. Alone, except for a bunch of doughnut-devouring strangers. Alone and wondering what the heck I was gonna cook for dinner.

✳ ✳ ✳

No, this can't be! What a sour twist of fate!
Thalia still thinks Dylan is her soul mate.
Well, shame on us and bully on her.
No more piddly games, it's time to make sure
That Dylan and Thalia are eternally severed.
Now here is the plan, which should part them forever.

Alek, you'll play Polly, and Era will be Tizzie.
You'll take Thalia out, and you'll keep her very busy
Then I'll become Thalia, bad shoes and all,
And wait for Apollo, no, Dylan, to call.

I'll trick dear Apollo into thinking I'm his,
He'll fly back to Olympus in a wink and a whiz,
Thinking his love won't be too far behind.
To our deception, they both will be blind,

✳ GODDESSES ✳

And poor little Thalia will be so heartbroken
To find Dylan has left, with no good-bye spoken.

Now, we can only do this trick one single time.
It zaps our powers, which is such a crime,
So concentrate, dear girls, this must work like a charm.
It's our last chance in this book to cause any real harm!

✳ ✳ ✳

SEVENTEEN

I had decided to just make bean burgers. I didn't dare try my hand at any more casserole surprises.

I was setting the table when I heard Polly and Era on the front porch, talking in low tones.

"Hey, what happened—why are you two home?" I called out.

"La, la, la, don't I look beautiful today?" asked Era in a singsong voice.

"What? Of course, always," I called out. "What happened to your survival class?"

"I survived!" declared Era.

"Oh, the class was canceled—we were so sad," Polly yelled from the living room.

I came out of the kitchen to see what was up. "What are you talking about? I thought you didn't even want to go. You were dreading it this morning," I said.

"No, that's what she means. We were thrilled, ecstatic," said Era. "Hey, you want to go get some ice cream, c'mon, please, please, please?"

"What? No, I don't want to get ice cream. Dylan is coming over for dinner, don't you remember? And when did you two start talking to each other, anyway? I thought today at the doughnut place, you said that was it, you were through with each other."

Polly said, "Oh, we made up. No, sisters shouldn't fight. Thalia, can you look into my eye? I think I might have something in it."

"I'm kinda busy here. Era, look at Polly's eye."

"I can't. Um, my hands are sticky from all the candy."

"Fine, let me wash *my* hands. And *I'm* supposed to be the selfish one? All right, Pol, come here."

"Right in this eye, look straight into it, can you see it?"

"I can't see anything," I said.

"Look straight into my eye, straight into my eye, you are feeling woozy."

"I feel woozy," I said.

"Now, weren't we on our way to get some soft serve?" said Era.

And Polly echoed, "Why, yes, I think that is something we all do deserve!"

EIGHTEEN

"I can't take it, I just can't take it," I moaned to no one in particular.

I was in the middle of the obstacle course, in the middle of the forest, in the middle of my long, torturous death. Me, Era, goddess of love poetry, a Muse, not to mention a pretty darn good-looking supreme being.

Miraculously I was a few paces ahead of Polly, but I didn't feel like a winner. My only solace, this hot pink sweatshirt I had borrowed from Thalia, was covered in mud. I could feel it cold against my belly. And my legs, they felt heavier than the weight of three plump leprechauns.* I couldn't lift them over another one of those stupid ropes.

Polly was probably fine, I thought bitterly. Sure. She was a little slower, but she liked this dirt stuff.

---

* Roughly 123 pounds.

Oh, my legs. They hurt and they were heavy and I didn't like them anymore.

And my hair, I couldn't even think of my hair. It was soggy. And heavy, too.

My legs. No more.

And then my legs, they gave out.

I sat there in a puddle of mud. Still wet, so cold and something far worse than tired. It made me more tired to think about how tired I was, and then, well, I couldn't help it. I started to cry.

I still had to go uphill for a mile and a half. There was no way I could make it. I cried harder. I wanted to do this for Polly and Thalia, I really did. I wanted to do this for my grade, to show Hera. I wanted to do this to get back home. But it was all gone. All my strength, all my energy, all my goddessness.

Except, well . . . no.

But no one was around.

No one would see.

I could muster up a little . . . magic.

I tried concentrating hard. It had been a while since I'd used my powers. I pressed my eyes closed tightly. I thought about yellow canaries and winged mice. The wind that had been whipping around pretty steadily suddenly whirled into a cone of tor-nadolike winds directly over my head.

I closed my eyes even tighter, willing the wind to take me up and over the course, to the other side. I'd just have to figure out how to fix my hair when I got there.

Suddenly my legs felt light as a feather. My bottom lifted off the ground ever so slightly. I felt that oh-so-familiar feeling of flotation. Levitation. Exaltation!

"Noooooooooooo!"

It was Polly.

Her horrifying scream threw my concentration south and my mini-tornado died, leaving me to hit the hard ground with a painful thump. I toppled over and fell deep into a puddle of sludgy mud.

Polly ran to my side.

I just cried louder.

"Era, no, no powers. C'mon, you can do this. Get up."

"I can't. You were right all along, this was a stupid idea."

"Yes, but the point is, we're here. And we've got to get through it, *without* our powers. If we don't, we haven't learned anything, and we have no hope of getting home. You can do this. I know you can. C'mon, let's just go slow, at our own pace, together. I'll help you."

"Really, you'll help me?"

"Well, I'm not going to carry you if that's what you're thinking, but yes, I will help you."

Rats, I thought. I continued to pout.

"You really thought I'd carry you?" Polly cried.

"Not carry, exactly. Maybe I could lean on you a little."

"C'mon. Let's go."

Everyone else was farther along than us. But that just meant fewer eyes to stare at us while we stumbled through the course. We trudged up the hill slowly, in unison. Each of Polly's steps seemed to inspire me to take one of my own.

"Concentrate on the trees, Era, not on your legs. . . ."

"Right, okay. Yes, the trees."

"Let's guess how old they are as we go, okay?"

"Okay, yes. One hundred sixteen."

"Two hundred twelve."

"Ninety-five."

It took our minds off the pain a little bit.

"Do you think we will ever get home, Pol?" I asked. The wind had died down. It was so quiet now, we could clearly hear a little tiny finch up in this tall elm nearby.

"Yes, yes, I do. Someday."

"Yeah, someday."

I stopped again. I felt like I was going to cry. It was just so much. I tried to think about the trees. I tried not to think about my legs or the pain, but I couldn't help it. I plopped down again in the dirt. I just didn't care.

Polly gave me a little pep talk.

"Look at you, my most 'indoor-minded' sister is out in the mud—that shows change."

"Yeah, but is it the right kind of change?" I was pouting, and I knew it.

"I think so. One step at a time, right?"

"Right."

And only twenty-three steps later (I wasn't counting or anything) we hit the top of the hill we had been climbing for what seemed like hours (but was probably only thirty minutes, thirty long minutes). We were shocked! And thrilled!

"Look, down there, Era, it's the finish line."

"There's Josh! And the others! Hallelujah, I'm not going to fail! I'm not going to die!"

"Of course not, silly. Hey, if you think you've got it in you, we could just barrel down this hill and . . ."

But before she'd even finished her sentence, she was off and running, propelled by the downhill slope and the rush of adrenaline. I got it, too, and I was off.

We sprinted (or sort of hobbled quickly) directly for that line like our immortality depended on it. I threw my hands out to the sides like I was flying. I actually felt good, I felt free! Polly practically skipped. Or maybe it was stumbling, but it looked vaguely like skipping.

Down and down and around a tree and another.

Quicker and quicker.

Faster and faster.

And through the finish line! We fell into each other's arms in the longest, squishiest hug we could find within our tired bodies.

Josh came over to congratulate us. He patted us both on the backs. And told us that despite being last in the class, we still deserved a big, fat A because we had accomplished our goals and completed the test.

And we both dropped to the ground in total exhaustion, just like that.

NINETEEN

Apollo, as Dylan, arrived at Thalia's door nervous and excited. His time spent on earth with Thalia had possibly been even better than his time spent in Olympus with her, as himself. Even the Furies hadn't been as much trouble as he'd expected here on earth. Although now that he'd thought about it, he realized they probably had had something to do with that disheartening camera incident.

But their tricks hadn't worked. That was the thing. He and Thalia were too good together, too strong together, to let even the Furies get in their way. Apollo grinned, shaking off the image of the evil ones. He was eager to see Thalia again, even under this ruse. And it only flattered him that she seemed so torn over liking him because he knew deep down, it was because of him. Because she felt like she was cheating on Apollo.

He stood outside Thalia's front door for a few moments, soaking in his life. He was three thousand years away from home, who knew how many miles, yet here he was, on the other side of a single door from his soul mate.

He took a deep breath and rang the bell.

Thalia came rushing to the door and dramatically threw open the screen.

Apollo noticed her left eye was twitching rather fast. Otherwise she looked perfect.

"Hi, you look really beautiful."

"Thank you," she said, grabbing him by the arm and ushering him inside. "Let me have your coat and sit down, please."

He was nervous, but in a good way. He sat down on the cushy floral couch in the living room. She came back into the living room and sat down close to him. Real close.

She smacked her gum, loud. And then said, "So, you wanna make out?"

"What? Thalia, you're acting weird—what's going on?"

"I mean, that's what you came over for, right? That's why I invited you. So how 'bout it?"

"Wait, not that I'm not flattered or intrigued, but you invited me here for dinner, right? And what about that boyfriend you have, the one back home?"

"I dumped him. I'm all yours."

"What? Why are you acting like this—what's going on?" Dylan stood up, a little dazed and a little confused.

"Oh, calm down. Jeez, I know it's you, Apollo, you can cut the Denver act."

"What? What do you mean?" he questioned. Dylan looked scared, nervous. He began to pace (a nervous habit).

"I'm messing with you. I've known all along that it was you or you were he or that, well, you know what I mean."

"You have?" he said as he threw his hands up in the air in shock.

"Yep, and I thought it was cute. And very sexy. Meow."

"You did?"

"Yep, and I'm ready to be Mrs. Apollo, forever and eternity. I mean, you stuck it out, even when I was a mean and nasty little Muse. I am seriously impressed with your dedication."

"You are?"

"Yes, now will you stop asking me all these silly doubting questions and kiss me?"

But he was still standing there in disbelief. Apollo had been sure Thalia didn't know who he really was.

Thalia ran over and jumped into his arms and laid a big wet one right on his lips. It was sloppier than he remembered, her lips weren't quite as soft, but was he really going to argue? This was the love of his life, right?

After she finished slobbering all over him, she said, "This is how I see it. You should go back home and tell Daddy I'm ready and willing. For real this time. No tricks. I'm sure Daddy will let me come home if I marry you."

"Well, actually, no, he said if I let on to my real identity, Hera would never let either of us back in Olympus again. Thalia, I can't go back."

"Nonsense! Father was just trying to scare ya. I'm sure he'll let me come home. Now just go on back home ASAP and tell him. I need to tidy up all my earth business down here, and then I will be up in a flash."

"I think he was very serious about Hera, Thalia. I don't know."

"That was just an act, to keep you in place. Hera's strong willed, but she's not evil. Now go home and tell Father!"

"Thalia, wait, it's just, I realize now I rushed you before. I was thinking we should date first. It would be a great honor. I don't want to force you into anything you're not ready for."

"Ready, schmeddy. Let's get married!"

"Are you sure about this?"

"As sure as my name is Thalia, silly. Now tell Father that the girls and I will be outside under the wild cherry blossom tree at one A.M. tomorrow night. We will be ready, our bags packed. He can beam us up then. Do you got that?"

"Well, yes, but . . ."

"No buts! Hurry along, I've got lots of packing to do."

"But what about dinner? What about my casserole surprise?" he asked.

"Trust me when I say this, you do *not* want to eat Thalia's cooking!"

He sort of half laughed. He had never heard Thalia talk about herself in the third person. He didn't really like it.

"Now kiss me, you fool!" she said, and she grabbed Apollo's neck, pulling him close to her, and kissed him hard on the lips. Then she blew a huge bubble gum bubble. Pop!

TWENTY

I woke up on our couch, in our living room, shivering. But all the windows were closed. I couldn't stop shaking. I was in a daze. And I could have sworn I'd heard a noise.

Oh goddess! How on earth had I fallen asleep right before my big dinner with Dylan? Could I have missed him? No, I couldn't have. It wasn't possible.

I jumped up and ran for the clock.

Whew. I was only asleep for a few minutes. It felt like eternity. I was supergroggy, like when you lick an ancient toad's left front foot.* I just couldn't warm up.

But Dylan was due anytime. I pulled myself together and threw the bean burgers in the toaster.

Funny thing was, I wasn't even hungry. I had had this dream about eating ice cream with Era and Polly, only they were being bratty—not like themselves, but

---

* Which by the way is sooo against the rules back home, but you can't help but try once or twice.

a little mean. I even felt like I had an ice cream tummy ache now. And the shivering wouldn't stop. Dreams are funny like that.

Maybe I'll toast the buns, I thought. I got them out of their bag and threw them in the toaster, too. I placed a hand on each side of the hot metal box. It wasn't warming me up, either.

Huh, he was now eleven minutes late. That was odd, wasn't it? Hmmm. No, I told myself not to be silly. I decided to get a sweater.

When the burgers were done and the buns were toasted, I put them on the plates. Surely he'd be here shortly. I'd already concocted a story about why my host parents were nowhere to be seen. I was going to tell him that they were on holiday in Uruguay. I saw Uruguay on the globe and thought it sounded like a great place to go. They were collecting seashells in Uruguay, yeah.

I went to the cold box and got out the ketchup, mustard, relish, and chocolate sauce for the burgers.

Hmmm, now he was twenty minutes late. The bean burgers were getting a little cold. I decided to just sit down and relax. I was a little nervous.

My tummy wasn't just full now, it was also a little sick. I had melancholy belly.

Fifteen minutes later and nothing. Okay, now I was really nervous. No word from him at all. Maybe he hurt himself. Tripped and fell over a sprinkler. Or walked into a tree. It could happen. Course he probably had that helmet on. He should be fine.

Sick. Sick. Sick.

Oh, oh, oh, I heard something. I ran to the door quicker than a dwarf being chased by a giant. But nothing. I looked outside. Nothing. I walked all the way around the house. Nothing. I ran up the street, to the corner. Nothing.

Over half an hour late now. *This is what Pocky calls being "stood up,"* I thought miserably. *He said it happens to him all the time.* But why would Dylan stand me up?

This didn't make any sense.

I really thought he liked me.

I really liked him.

I really needed to puke.

TWENTY-ONE

Three days later and a million miles away . . .

Apollo sat in Zeus's chamber, his head in his hands. He felt weak and tired. The journey back to Olympus had taken a toll on his body and his mind. Once home, it was the wait that just about killed him.

"She wasn't there, Apollo, the girls weren't under the tree at one, not today, not yesterday, not the day before that. My daughter has once again played you and me for fools!"

"This can't be—I don't believe it. Perhaps this is just another one of your glitches," Apollo boldly suggested.

"How dare you! I don't make glitches. Just slight and slim slips. This is most certainly not my doing. Even the Furies themselves report no sign of them stirring."

"And you believe those little witches?"

"It is not for me to question—"

"Yes! Yes, it is for you to question. They're untrustworthy freakish finks! They are exceptionally evil and most monstrously mad. You can't possibly believe them?"

"I have nothing that proves them to be saying anything fake, faux, or fictitious."

"They could've used their own magic to keep the girls from the wild cherry blossom tree. Maybe they physically stopped the girls! Blocked their way! Put a spell on them!"

"Nonsense. That is just wishful thinking on your part, Apollo. The evidence speaks alone here, young man. If you have anything, any shred of evidence that can provide any sort of explanation, please, bring it forth now. Otherwise just go."

"But sir," begged Apollo.

"Nothing, then? You have nothing? I can't look at you any longer. Do you know I have the hall reserved for your wedding already? I had to bump Pygmalion and Galatea a week from Thursday to open it up for you and my deceitful daughter. This is all most upsetting."

"Well, I have to say, Thalia was acting strange, very oddly, on that final day," recalled Apollo. He was shaking his head hard, trying to remember all the details.

"Oddly how?" asked Zeus, who was truly interested in getting to the bottom of this mess.

"Well, she was rather pushy."

"Oh, please, Thalia is always pushy," Zeus said, and threw his hands in the air.

"No, not pushy, exactly. She was very, um, how do I say this delicately?"

"Delicate, schmelicate, say it, boy," bellowed Zeus.

"She was very impudent. She was, um, rather affectionate. She was kissy, sir."

"That's what you've got? Pshaw! If she was trying to convince you she was in love with you, wouldn't she act that way? This is nothing, you have nothing. Go!"

"No, you don't understand. Thalia may be bold in her manner, but not when it comes to these matters. I know her. Something wasn't right."

"Yes, and I daresay that something was you. She obviously is having the time of her life down there and wants nothing to do with home. She will get her wish. You are forbidden to return to earth, and she is forbidden to come back to Olympus until her attitude changes drastically. This is my final word on this matter. Now, leave."

"But I know it, I know something was not right. Her lips, they weren't nearly as soft, her breath wasn't nearly so sweet . . . in fact, it was rather stinky."

"Leave! At once!"

"But . . ."

"Now!"

"Yes, O noble and honorable and handsome sir," said Apollo.

"Flattery will not work this time. . . . Apollo, don't let the chamber door hit you in the behind."

But it did. And it hurt.

TWENTY-TWO

"Do you want half of my banana-and-peanut-butter-sandwich?" It was Polly, trying to feed me.

"No thanks, I'm not hungry."

"But you haven't been hungry since that boy left town. We're going on four days now—you've got to eat more than the occasional grape."

"I know, I'm just really not hungry."

Claire was having lunch with us, too, in the quad. "Well, you can't possibly say no to a vegan torta with avocado, soy mayo, soy cheese, salsa, tomatoes, and sprouts, can you?" Claire had gone vegetarian when I wasn't looking. She and Polly had bonded over it. "Eat it now!" Claire demanded.

It was really good. But I still felt crummy.

In fact, I felt worse than crummy. The Fates were messing with me. They had played some cruel, sick joke on me. I had real feelings for some weird mortal named Dylan from Denver, but I was getting karmic payback for the lousy way I'd treated Apollo. And Apollo, I felt crazy sick over him, too. The guilt had caught up with me, and now I couldn't move much. How could I have done this? I had two wonderful guys in my life, and I pushed one away while the other ran, and fast. I was selfish. Selfish and horrible and I deserved everything I had coming to me and more.

I would've, should've spent the last three days since Dylan stood me up sleeping, but I was too scared of what my dreams might hold. What evil punishments and weird ice cream trips they would bring. So I'd been awake, thinking, pondering what went wrong, for hours upon hours upon hours (three whole days' worth). I hadn't come up with much. Other than that selfish thing.

"What are you thinking about, Thal?" asked Era. I guess I had gone off into a daze.

"That dream. That weird dream."

"Not the dream again. You're going to make your-self crazy," Polly said softly.

"It was just so real. I mean, you two, you said the obstacle course test was canceled. And then we went out for ice cream. What if the dream was related to his disappearance?"

"It was a dream, sweetie. You've got to let it go," said Era.

"They're right," added Claire. "I have realistic dreams all the time. Like in last night's dream, I kissed weird little Marc Banks and then I got on a bus with a llama."

We all sort of smiled. Even me.

"You know," she said, "that Marc guy can really kiss. What flavor ice cream did you have?"

"Mint chip."

"Well, you see, we can analyze this," claimed Claire. "Now, had you said 'vanilla,' I would say your subconscious was trying to tell you that you didn't like Dylan at all. Had you answered 'strawberry,' I could say that you felt he was the sweetest guy that ever lived and you were head over heels. But since you said 'mint chip,' I'm gonna translate that dream to mean that you were mixed up about him. See, the chips represent little obstacles, aka little droplets of doubt, in a big mound of tingling, aka love, the mint."

"Oh, please," I said, wondering if that was true.

Even so, I couldn't help but wonder if the dream was the key to understanding what went wrong. It was just so real.

"Okay, lunch over," declared Claire. "That bell's gonna ring in five, four, three, two, one . . ."

Dong. Dong.

"C'mon, Thalia, let's get to Media," beckoned Claire.

I solemnly bid my sisters adieu and we headed for class.

"I just don't understand, Claire. How did a football player disappear into thin air?"

"I told you already, Thal, he didn't disappear. His folks picked up and moved again. Back home to Denver, according to the school office."

"Yeah, but it's just so odd."

"I know. But there will be other guys . . . maybe not as klutzy as Dylan, but there will be more."

"Yeah." But I didn't want other guys. I wanted Dylan.

We walked into class.

"Class, sit down, please. I have an announcement." It was Mrs. Tracy.

"I am very pleased to say, most of your films were exceptional. Most."

Oh, great, it looked like she was staring directly at me when she said that. This would be the topper to my unsuccessful first and only attempt at romance on earth. I was also going to get an F. Hades, here I come!

"Yes, they were mostly good. But the film that stands out in my mind the most is one that really bucked the system. These two students turned lemons into lemonade when they broke their camera, and we'll be discussing that part more later, but they came through and turned in a fantastic commentary on teenage life today with their own video camera.

"Thalia, your project with Dylan brought tears to my eyes. I thought it was very advanced for such young souls, and I'm honored to be your teacher. I only wish Dylan were here to share in this joy and this A-plus."

"Me too," I mumbled. Still, I had to be happy about the grade. I was saved, for now.

"I've decided to send your film off to the Georgia Film Festival. I will keep the whole class informed on your progress. Thank you for such a fine piece of work."

"Um, you're welcome."

All this talk of Dylan and the movie just made me more upset. I couldn't concentrate. I started shaking again, shivering. The dream. It had to be the dream. Mrs. Tracy dimmed the lights to begin showing the class movies so we could talk about them out loud.

I sank deep in my chair and pulled out the note.

It was a piece of paper that I found in my locker the day after I was "stood up."

It was the only thing I had of his.

I unfolded the paper for the twenty-third time and read it again.

Thalia,
    You make me so mad sometimes. And so very happy. Most of all you make me laugh.

I just wanted to let you know how special you truly are and how much this has meant to me.

By the time you read this, I'll be home.

Till you are with me . . .

XO

It took twenty-three readings, but I finally understood. I knew there was something in this note. Some sort of hidden message.

Dylan wants me to come to Denver!

IF YOU THOUGHT THIS
BOOK WAS GOOD, TAKE
A SNEAK PEEK AT
GODDESSES 3,
MUSES ON THE MOVE

ONE

Monday, 4:00 P.M., front counter of the local café, the Grind

"A caffé latte for Polly, I'll have a single shot of espresso, and hey, Era, what do you want?"

"An extra-large mocha. With whipped cream. And sprinkles, those chocolate ones," she said.

I turned to the exasperated girl behind the counter and continued our order. "And an extra large mocha with whipped cream and sprinkles. Claire, Pocky, what do you want?"

"A chai soy latte for me," said Claire.

"I just want a Coke, thanks, Thalia—oh, and a muffin, one of those giant muffins. And an oatmeal cookie, too, please," said Pocky.

I turned back to the girl and placed the rest of the order, meeting her dirty look with my own bitter scowl. Then I plopped down on the couch with my sisters, Claire, and Pocky to wait for our drinks. I was in a foul mood.

Why? Well, for one thing, Dylan from Denver had disappeared into thin air. One day we were friends, maybe even more than friends, and then poof! He was gone, out of my life. As if I haven't already had enough of the "poof, good-bye" stuff. As in, "Poof, good-bye, Olympus," "Poof, good-bye, Daddy, and most of my sisters and everyone I've ever known," as in, "Poof, good-bye, Apollo."

Another thing getting my goat was that we hadn't heard from Daddy lately or from his messenger, Hermes. And we were all coming along splendidly in the challenges he had given us, so we were expecting to get word any day—telling us our banishment was over and we could come back home. Polly was actually learning to mind her own business and stick by her convictions (as in, not letting me talk her into anything bad). Era was becoming a strong, independent young woman instead of a boy-crazy dreamer with no willpower. And I was . . . um . . . working on it. *It* being my selfishness.

"So, girls, what've you all got planned for the Thanksgiving holiday?" asked Claire. Her formerly purple hair was now dark and tipped in yellow, a color perfectly matched to her favorite eye shadow.

Before Polly or I had a chance to come up with an acceptable mortal answer to that question, Era chimed in, all curls and smiles. "What's Thanksgiving?"

"You're kidding—you guys don't know about

Thanksgiving?" questioned Pocky, like we were three total freaks (albeit three very fashionably dressed and cute girl freaks).

I have to say, I was mortified. But then Claire jumped in. "Oh, silly me, of course you don't know about Thanksgiving since you girls are from Europe. It's a totally American holiday."

"Oh, right," I muttered, thankful for that we're-exchange-students-from-Europe story we told when we first arrived here in Athens, Georgia.

"Wait—holiday? Does that mean we get days off from school? Like how many?" asked Era, thrilled by the prospect of some time away from Nova High.

"Yeah, we get a four-day weekend—everyone does."

"I love Thanksgiving!" cried Era.

Suddenly I felt my bad mood drifting away. Four days away from homework. Four days away from the rumors that are always circulating about me and my sisters and how weird we are. Most importantly, four days away from the Furies. The Furies, who never let us forget they're here, that they're three strong complete *with* magic, that they're powerful and they're watching us, waiting for the slightest mistake to send them tattling to our evil, might I even say ugly, stepmother, Hera. "Four days without the Backroom Betties!" I said enthusiastically.

Our drinks arrived by way of yet another snooty-looking Grind employee. We all fell silent.

After the gal left, I broached the subject casually. "So, tell me more about this Thanksgiving thing. You Americans have so many cool, um, holidays."

"Okay, so like, back about four hundred years ago, way long ago, a bunch of people in funny hats came to America, well, to Plymouth Rock, supposedly, to escape religious persecution," said Claire. "So they got here and, well, the Indians were already here. They decided to join them in a dinner party to celebrate this new country."

"No, no, no, that's not what Thanksgiving is about," complained Pocky. Pocky was a little taller and a little thinner than everyone else at school. But he made it even more noticeable by wearing his orange hair in a mohawk as tall as it would go and his clothes as big and baggy as he could get away with without them falling around his ankles.

Pocky continued. "Thanksgiving is all about food and, okay, giving thanks for those good things in your life, but mostly it's about food. Like a big golden turkey and mashed potatoes and gravy and sweet potatoes with marshmallows and—"

"Leave it to you, Pocky, to see the holiday as a food fest," Claire interrupted disapprovingly.

"Yeah, well, this year I don't get any of that," he said, sulking. "My parents are going to Barbados and leaving me at home alone. They thought by throwing some cash my way, it would make it all better. But

no, it doesn't. No sweet potatoes. No pie. No turkey."
He was almost in tears.

"I wish my parents would throw some cash at me and be on their way," said Claire. "I requested that this year they perhaps try making something, I dunno, less cruel. I just can't sit at that dinner table while my brother and father tear at that poor defenseless turkey like it was their last meal on earth. But noooooo, Mom just laughed at me."

"Maybe we should celebrate Thanksgiving together, Claire," said Polly, who always agrees with Claire's feelings about animals. You know, if Polly had been born an animal instead of a goddess, I'd say she would've been a graceful swan because she's got all the beauty and poise of a long-necked bird.

"Or maybe we should take advantage of the four-day weekend and go somewhere we've never been!" I yelped suddenly, before the thought had barely enough time to form in my brain. *Like Denver!* Luckily I kept *that* thought from escaping my lips.

"Yes, yes! I want to go to the chocolate factory—where is that, exactly?" asked Era of no one in particular.

"No, no," said sensible Polly, her eyes looking downward. I think she was trying to communicate to us that we should have this discussion later, when we were alone. But we ignored her.

"You guys should go on a trip. A road trip!" encouraged Claire.

"Yes, a road trip!" I cried, although I didn't know what that meant.

"Wait, you guys don't have a car—what was I thinking?" said Claire.

Oh, a road trip involved a car. A trip to anywhere involved a car. The thought brought back my bitter mood. The *Furies* had a car. A big one—something people call a minivan. It was an ugly, horrid shade of pink—at least that made me feel better. But still, Daddy could have at least given us a—

"I have a car," said Pocky with all the enthusiasm of a Roman fairy* amped up on sugar pellets.

Now my sister Polly's eyes were huge and angry and raging blue. I could tell from her disapproving side glances that she didn't like the idea in the first place and now, the thought that Pocky, a mortal, might join us for four whole days nonstop? I think that just made her livid.

"But wait, what about your host parents, guys?" asked Claire.

Polly started to say, "That's right," but I interrupted her and said that our host parents (ahem, our *imaginary* host parents) hated holidays in general and would be happy to have the house to themselves for a weekend.

Era cried out, "Yes!" Her thin, long fingers danced in the air.

"I can't believe I haven't had a chance to meet them yet," Claire replied. "They sound so wacky."

---

* They're annoyingly perky but fun to hang out with if you're in the right mood.

Polly just sank lower and lower in the deep, furry brown couch. She couldn't fight us, at least not in here, in the dark space of the Grind with all these people around. Plus, it was two to one. Three to one if you counted Pocky.

"So when do we leave?" I blurted out, changing the subject. Besides, I had a lot of planning to do, and I wanted to get started. I'd have to figure out how to get to Denver. Then I'd have to decide how to break it to my sisters that I wanted, no, *needed* this road trip to take me there.

"Well, we can leave right after school on Wednesday. It's a half day, so we're out by noon," said Pocky. "And I have to be back by Sunday afternoon to pick up my parents from the airport."

"Right. Okay, then, it's settled—we leave Wednesday." That was only two days away. I shivered. A happy shiver.

"I wish I could go with you!" cried Claire.

"I wish you could come, too, Claire," I said.

"Well, I'll be thinking of you guys while I sit there in front of the poor, dead stuffed bird."

"Oh, speaking of that," said Pocky, "I'll go anywhere you girls want to go since you're our foreign guests and all. My only request is that on Thanksgiving Day, I get some turkey—sorry, Claire. And mashed potatoes and gravy and stuffing and, let's see, cranberry sauce and pie. . . ."

"Fair enough," I agreed, jerking my head up and

down. "Anything you say, Pocky. Anything." Pocky, Claire, and Era gave me weird looks. Polly just closed her eyes and rubbed her forehead miserably.

But c'mon, how could I contain my enthusiasm? Four days away from the Furies? Four days on a real live earth adventure? A chance to see Dylan and figure out my true feelings for him?

That, my friend, would be worth all the pie in Georgia.

❋ ❋ ❋

Oh, dear Muses, can you be so naive?
We Furies would follow you beyond Tel Aviv,
Those are Hera's orders, for it was us three she chose
To torment you on earth—from your heads to your toes.
We heard you speak loosely and wildly of a trip
As we hid in a corner, nibbling cheddar cheese dip,
You've used your powers, and for that you will pay,
But in the meantime more fun's on the way.
We don't know how, but we'll come up with a scam
To turn your vacation into a shim and a sham,
Yes, we swear on our hairstyles and our mauve minivan
that we'll make a mockery of your Thanksgiving plan!

❋ ❋ ❋

Two

Back in Olympus, on the tippy top of Mount Samaras

Many miles and years away, Apollo waited for Zeus on the top of the flattest mountain in Olympus. They had a tennis game scheduled, but Zeus was a no-show.

Apollo wasn't in the mood for a game, anyway. He hadn't been in the mood for much of anything since Thalia had duped him into coming back to Olympus alone. All that begging Zeus for a chance to help the Muses, all that running around disguised as a football player, and for what? For Thalia to break his heart all over again.

He had stopped playing his lyre.* He had stopped going on adventures. He had stopped fighting crime. All of his favorite things.

In fact, the sun had not set in days, and it was all Apollo's fault.** But Apollo had neither the will nor

---

* A harplike thing that Apollo used to play day and night. It really bothered many of his god neighbors, but they didn't dare say a word.

** The sun was stubborn and stayed where it wanted to until the hunky and powerful Apollo rode his chariot by and demanded the sun set or rise.

the energy to even *pet* his horses, let alone command them to gallop through the skies.

Even his own twin sister, Artemis,* couldn't rouse him for archery or a good game of golf. No, Apollo was down and out. Devastated. Depressed. Things were dire.

It was quite shocking, really, that he had in fact shown up for the scheduled tennis match. But he was curious. He wanted to see if Zeus had any news about Thalia. He couldn't stop caring. In fact, he really didn't want to.

When he realized Zeus wasn't coming, part of him wanted to go back home to his own small castle in the clouds and bury his head in his silver satin sheets. But the bigger part of him had to know about Thalia. So he went to Zeus's very large castle in hopes of hearing something, anything, about his love.

A sprinkle of dust and he was in the castle's dark and cavernous waiting room. Most of the castle was bright and cheery, but Zeus had purposefully created this room to be as ugly and torturous as possible. He was the all-powerful and mighty Zeus, and he had a reputation to uphold.

Apollo looked around for servants, but none appeared. And then he realized why. That screaming. That high, shrill, evil voice. It would scare anyone away. Anyone who wasn't determined to find out at least a nugget of information about the girl they loved.

Apollo crept up the stairs toward the noise. Eight doors down on the right he found the source. It was coming from Thalia's old bedroom.

---

* His loving virgin twin sis who spent her days getting out her frustrations by killing wild beasts.

He pressed his ear to the door (and he really didn't have to—when Hera screamed, all of Olympus heard).

"I don't care, Zeus, the girls have used their powers again! They broke *my* rules. . . . They're done for!"

"Now, Hera, be reasonable. They've been getting very good grades in that mortal high school, right? Era even got a B in some survival class! And Thalia, her movie got an A-plus!" Zeus's voice sounded very desperate.

Apollo was delighted to hear that his film project with Thalia had scored her a perfect grade. That had to count for something.

"Grades?" Hera snorted. "I don't *really* care about grades. I didn't send them down there to get an education, I sent them there to punish them for being evil little children who don't know their place in society."

"But Hera, you were the one who made it a condition that they get good grades!"

"Oh, I don't care if they win the National Science Award. I just wanted to give them headaches. They're rotten little scoundrels. They deserve to rot in Hades,* and that's just where I intend to send them!"

"*No!* Now, Hera, be reasonable—you are not sending my beautiful girls to Hades. I'm putting my foot down. No."

"I don't care where you put your foot. I gave them rules for their life on earth, and they broke them. The Furies have reported that they have used their magic freely!"

Apollo crumpled to the floor. Sitting there, so far

---

* In essence the god hell. It was an ugly, dirty, abominable place, unfortunately ruled by the dastardly evil three, the Furies.

from Thalia and her sisters, he felt even more help-less, if that were possible. Apollo continued to listen.

"No, they didn't use it freely, Hera, honey bunny, they used it in bits, and my God, they went from liv-ing with magic daily to cold turkey, no magic! I love you, my sweet, but what do you expect?"

"I expect respect. I expect grace and dignity, and I expect that I don't have to worry about my own step-daughters turning me green! I expect you to let me handle this situation, and I expect you to continue helping me with this harp—my music recital starts in just three hours!"

"Look, dear, sweetums, I will give you respect, but I will not let you send my girls to Hades. No, they haven't been that bad. Well, outside of that horrible little Apollo debacle."

Apollo's ears went red. His heart burned so fiercely, his arms just dropped to his side, lifeless.

"Yes, well, I wasn't too keen, Zeus, about your deci-sion to send Apollo down there in disguise, but it all worked out in the end, now, didn't it? Thalia proved herself to be simply wretched yet again." And then she added, "Apollo got what he deserved!" It stung his ears like a hundred and one bees. He could hear the smile on Hera's face.

"Yes, my little chickadee, well, I was very disap-pointed in her for that, yes."

"Then let's get her and get her good. To Hades!"

And at that moment the hallway went black, a wicked wind whipped through the space where Apollo was sitting, and he felt cold, wet, and chilly.

"NO!" Zeus bellowed.

And the wind stopped.

"Zeus, listen to me and listen good. I set the rules for this game; therefore, I get to punish the girls when they break them. It's out of your hands, it's god's laws . . . but I tell you what. I'm so convinced that they will break my rules again, that they will use their magic freely and they will never fulfill your silly challenges without it, that I'm willing to give them one more chance before I send them to Hades. One more. But I tell you, dear, as I stand before you, they are going down. Straight down to the darkest depths of eternal damnation—they are going to Hades." And then her infamous cackle rang out through the whole castle, throughout all of Olympus, probably throughout all of Greece below.

Zeus was quiet. Apollo couldn't move. He knew he could be found out for listening in and would probably be punished severely, but he couldn't pick himself up. He pictured Thalia in Hades, cleaning up after the dreaded Furies, doing their laundry and their wicked deeds, and he slowly stood up, clenching his fists.

"I can't . . . I can't . . . I can't get involved," he said aloud to no one but himself. "Thalia's pushed me away for the very last time."